In The JAR

A Novel of Ireland

RONALD E. GAFFNEY

CONTENTS

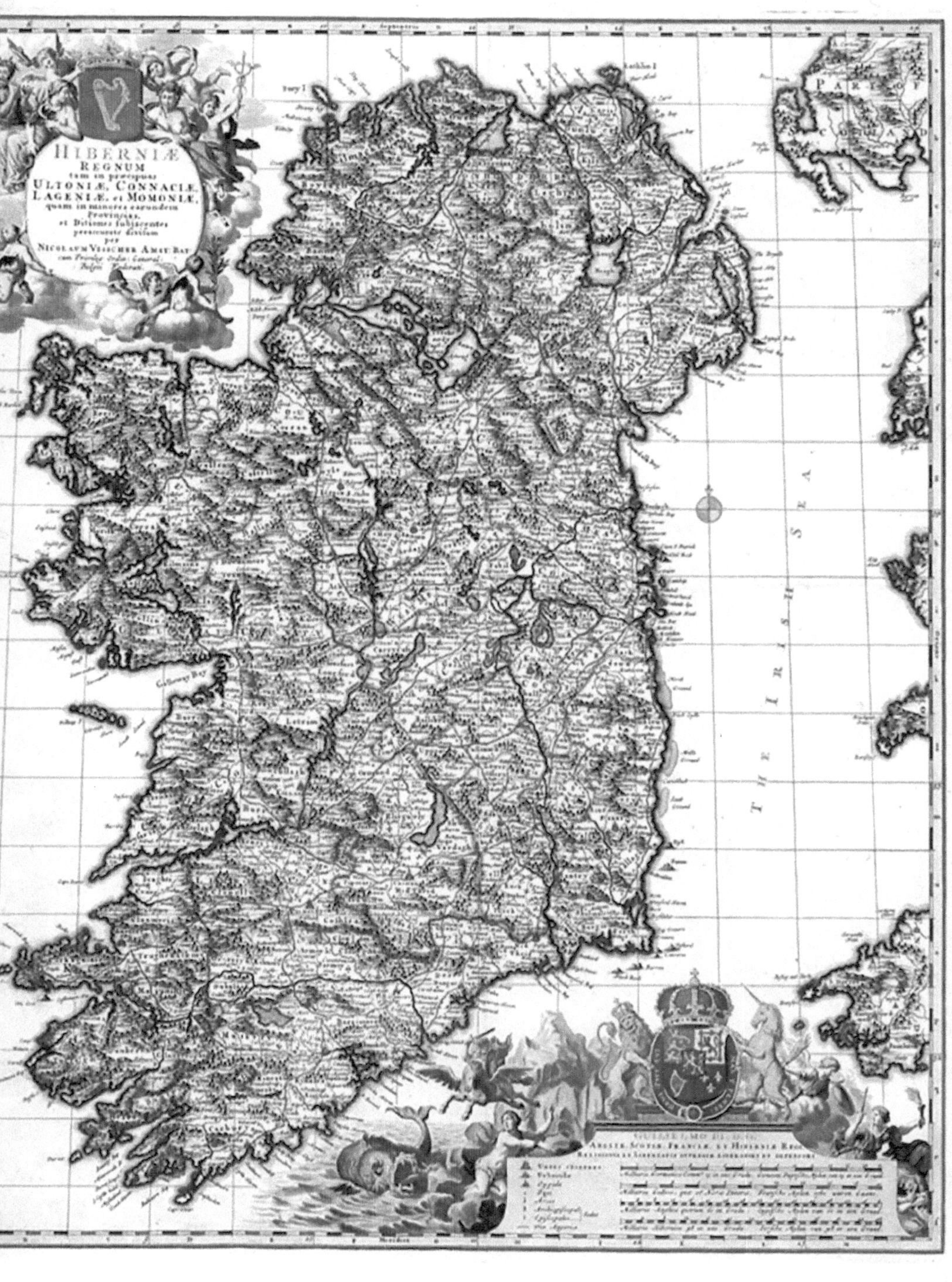

HIBERNIÆ
REGNUM
tam in præcipuas
ULTONIÆ, CONNACIÆ,
LAGENIÆ, et MOMONIÆ,
quam in minores earundem
Provincias,
et Ditiones subjacentes
percommode divisam
per
NICOLAUM VISSCHER AMST. BAT.
cum Privilegio Ordin. General.
Belgii Fœderati.

Introduction

Eighteenth Century Ireland: A country seething with civil unrest and lawlessness. After failed wars and rebellions against a rapidly expanding English rule, the Irish, stifled by the "Penal Laws" introduced by the Irish parliament and "Protestant Ascendancy". Pushed back with acts of murder, robbery and insurrectionist plotting - especially in the rebellious counties in the south and southwest of the island.

Enter our protagonist, Patrick Finn, son of the one of Ireland's "Wild Geese" who retired to France with the treaty of Limerick in 1691. Raised in the household of a Franco-Irish Aristocrat, Patrick served in the "Irish Brigade" in the service of France and found himself among the prisoners taken by the British after the battle of Culloden in Scotland in April 1746. Returned to France by the British, Patrick elects to make his way to Ireland - A homeland he has never seen - following in the footsteps of his older brother, John, who was at odds with the rest of his family over the very fact and benefits of British rule in Ireland.

While Patrick begins his Irish return in a lawful occupation, he soon becomes enamoured with the lives of the "Highwaymen" who stalked Ireland's country roads and became legends as "Rapparees" striking fear into the hearts of local English and Irish officials and lan downer. Being Hailed as a hero by the rebellious Irish common folk, and putting his military skills to good use, Patrick roamed the Irish backcountry looking for unsuspecting travellers in order to relieve them of their purses, paying special attention to Englishmen in transit and the Irish gentry and aristocrats who abided them. Patrick also became enamoured with one Ginny O'Neill, barmaid and friend to the male patrons of the "Black Horse Inn", where she worked and where Patrick kept a room.

Running afoul of a local landowner and tax collector, Patrick is jailed but promptly escapes and then must flee after commiting an unspeakable crime.

Loosely based on the tale spun in the Irish folk tune "Whiskey In The Jar", Our Story provides some historical context for the rise of the legendary Irish "Highwaymen" who robbed the rich, won a small fortune, risked it all and gave Irish men and women pride in those rakes who bedevilled their occupiers.

1. Wild Geese

SAINT-ANDRÉ, FRANCE, 15TH OF JUNE 1735.

"If you choose to leave, do not darken my door ever again," my father said, his voice rising with each word he spoke. The whole house seemed to shake with his angry outburst. He was now at the very end of his patience with my rebellious brother.

"Do not concern yourself with me. I will not be coming back here to a house full of idolaters and priest-ridden sheep. Goodbye, Father," my brother, John, declared in a heated but measured tone. He stormed out, pulling our chateau's front door shut behind him.

Raised in what was ostensibly an Irish Catholic household in Saint-André, France, my older brother chafed under a religion and associated political beliefs that he found objectionable and oppressive. He had resolved to return to his ancestral homeland, Ireland, to help with its rebuilding in a more enlightened and progressive manner than he had been exposed to during his upbringing. He was determined to adopt a new life, new views, and a new religion while serving Protestant overlords who he felt had a more informed view of the world than his kin. With his change in residence would come a change in his allegiance as well: he planned to swear an oath of loyalty to the alleged King of Great Britain and Ireland, George II.

I say "alleged" as our family—save for John—were all unapologetic Catholic "Jacobites." They supported King James II when he ascended to the English throne in 1685 and continued their support even when his daughter joined in a bid with her Dutch Protestant husband, William of Orange, to seize control of the English throne. James, a Catholic convert, had initially supported the adherents to the Church of England in their control of English politics and government. He tried to walk a very fine line between his adopted religion and English Protestant governance. But as time went by, he began to insert known Catholics into the military. He appointed them to high office while pushing the principle of 'religious tolerance' as an example to the nation. That approach proved to be too much for a conservative, Protestant-dominated Parliament to abide: the English "invited" the renowned Protestant warrior defender on the continent, William of Orange, and his wife, Mary, to rule as 'joint sovereigns.' William took up the invitation, and with a fleet and army larger than the Spanish Armada, he invaded the south coast of England from the continent. Parliament did nothing to defend the realm, save for deposing the very king God had seen fit to place on their throne. In 1688, they joyously welcomed William and Mary to rule over the English nation in a "Glorious Revolution."

James II eventually fled to Ireland and convened a rival Irish parliament to proclaim himself the 'true' king of the British realms. The Catholic aristocracy and the Irish army rallied to his cause, and he attempted to subdue Protestant plantations and strongholds loyal to William, such as the city of Derry in the north of Ireland, but with no success. Derry rebuffed James's siege, and William pursued James to Ireland, where he defeated his forces at the Battle of the Boyne in July of 1690. James's Irish supporters then retreated to the south of the country, determined to make a stand. My father, known as "Red Thomas" O'Finn, was among those in the army and had fought at the Boyne. He was the son of a substantial Irish Catholic landowner from the west of Ireland and was determined not to bow to these recent Protestant invaders or accept William as his king. Meanwhile, James II fled to the continent under the protection and patronage of King Louis XIV of France.

The Irish army, under the command of Patrick Sarsfield, established a strong defensive line along the Shannon River and repelled several attempts by William's forces to advance into the south and west of the country. Based at Limerick, with a second force at Galway, the Jacobite's 20,000-man army, however, could not be sustained by the local populations, leading both the military and civilians to starve for food and essential supplies. Consequently, Limerick came under siege by William's forces in the late summer of 1690. The Protestant attackers encircled the town and breached Limerick's stout walls with their artillery. Yet, they encountered interior earthworks and well-erected barricades. Danish grenadiers and eight regiments of troops who followed them were decimated by intense musket and cannon fire and were forced to withdraw. The siege was lifted, celebrated by the Catholic defenders as the fulfillment of an old Irish prophecy promising a great Irish victory at Limerick. Unfortunately, the following year, a second siege of Limerick by William's forces resulted in a stalemate and a treaty of surrender involving the Catholic defenders.

William and James both viewed the ongoing fighting in Ireland as a mere distraction, draining valuable resources from their main efforts on the battlefields of Europe, aimed at delivering decisive blows to each other. It was finally agreed between the parties to allow the Jacobite army to leave Ireland with their arms, flags, baggage, wives, and children and sail to France to serve under King Louis. By the Treaty of Limerick in 1691, 14,000 Irish troops accepted the offer and retired with 6,000 family members in tow, an event often referred to as the "Flight of the Wild Geese" in popular lore. My father and mother were among these "geese." A few thousand soldiers chose to remain and serve under their former enemy, William, while a few thousand more were simply allowed to return home. Although civil articles signed with the Jacobites guaranteed religious tolerance in Ireland and the preservation of large Catholic estates, in practice, Catholics faced numerous new legal disabilities. The lands of the departed and others were soon confiscated, and many Irish leaders were designated as wanted outlaws and criminal outcasts.

While the large clashes of armies were at an end in Ireland, the supporters of William now found themselves confronted by 'irregulars' raiding and robbing their forces in the name of James II – the so-called "Rapparees" (or "Stabbers" in English), also known by some as "Tories" (from the Irish word for "pursuers"). These sons of Ireland, sometimes lone individuals, resorted to ambush and stealth to strike at William's forces after the major battles had concluded in 1691. It's true that over time, some Rapparees turned to criminal activities to feed and supply themselves and their supporters. Unfortunately, their crimes sometimes affected both Catholics and Protestants alike. In previous wars, English forces responded to the Rapparees by depopulating entire rebellious areas, such as the Wicklow Mountains, and destroying everything that could sustain the irregular bands. English forces were then free to kill anyone found in these restricted areas, whether guilty or innocent, and they did so. At one point, the Roman Catholic population of Dublin was largely removed from the city on the belief that they were somehow aiding the local rebels with food, support, and information.

While many "Tories" eventually left for France at the end of earlier wars, others stayed on, dispersed, but later reconstituted their bands when James II arrived in Ireland. Lacking arms and supplies, many Rapparees were forced to find their resources and resorted to attacking and pillaging William's supply caches, camps, castles, and the fringes of his army. These raiders tied down thousands of William's regular troops, who had to protect their supply lines. The Rapparees proved to be of great assistance to the army of James II. However, with the "Flight of the Wild Geese" and violent English efforts to quell all forms of insurrection in Ireland, some Rapparees again left for the continent, were caught and executed, or simply blended into local populations, emerging opportunistically to strike against the occupiers. The English referred to these fighters who stayed behind as "highwaymen," rogues, and criminal rabble, but most were simply Jacobites determined to make life for the English in Ireland and their Irish allies as miserable as possible.

One might wonder, "How did a prince from a German state – the Hanoverian George I – eventually come to ascend the English throne following William of Orange?" The English Parliament began to worry when William and Mary produced no heir and were succeeded on the throne by the last Anglican member of the Stuart line, Queen Anne

– who was also the half-sister of James Edward Stuart, the Catholic-raised son of James II. In the absence of a surviving heir from Anne (which did not occur), the possibility of a Catholic Stuart returning to the throne became real. Determined to keep the throne in Protestant hands, Parliament enacted legislation in 1701 to subsequently place only Protestants (in this case, George I, a distant Protestant relative of James II) in the line of succession to rule over England, Ireland, and Scotland. This move, along with the union of Scotland with England in 1707, triggered several Scottish Jacobite rebellions – all of which the English swiftly and mercilessly crushed. George I was succeeded on the throne by George II in 1727. It was to this German prince that my brother, John, intended to transfer his loyalty. The English had already taken to calling James II and all those in the Catholic Stuart line "pretenders" to the throne of England, but my father and I considered William, and later the various Protestant "Georges" who followed him, to be the real pretenders.

John, my brother, two years my senior, and I were raised in Saint André, France, a small town in the north-central part of that country. We lived at the Chateau de Saint-André, a noble estate granted to my father by Louis XIV as a reward for his exceptional military service to the French crown and the Catholic cause, both in Ireland and on the battlefields of Europe. I, Patrick Finn, was born at the estate's chateau in 1715. John and I had one other younger sibling, Erin, who was very close to our long-suffering mother, Patricia.

John and I enjoyed exceptional childhoods, freely roaming over our vast estate while our father was away fighting for the king. As we ran and hid among the forests, along the streams, and behind the hedges around the chateau, John and I fancied ourselves, mythical Irish warrior heroes, like Cu Chulainn or the Irish King Brian Boru, defeating invading Norsemen. As we grew older, we rode the estate's horses on the surrounding highways and through the nearby fields, both becoming accomplished horsemen. We bonded during these early days of freedom and grew close, determined to always support one another. "I will always be at your back," John declared. "And I at yours," I replied. Our blood and emotional ties were strong.

We were both educated by a tutor, and I firmly believe that this schooling gave rise to many of our family's later problems. Our tutor, Monsieur Pierre Dupont, followed the teachings of many of the current French philosophers and became a fervent opponent of the "Divine Right of Kings" and the principles of absolutism. He was a secularist, a radical, and probably an atheist, and had our father known about his beliefs, he would have driven him off the estate at the point of a sword. I found the tutor's views to be rather strange, even laughable at times and rejected them outright. However, John took Dupont's sometimes subtly imparted messages to heart. He began to believe that only 'enlightened' monarchs responsible to the elected representatives of the people should rule. As a result, John and Father began to clash more and more frequently over religion and politics, with the air growing tense whenever the two were together. Booming voices and the sound of slamming doors frequently filled the chateau as Father and Son confronted one another. Father began to spend less time at home as a result of these conflicts, hoping to quell John's growing alienation through his absences, but it did not work.

The feud between father and son undoubtedly put a strain on our mother – as if she had not suffered enough already over the years. She grew up on tales of slaughtered relatives during Oliver Cromwell's nearly five-year ravaging of Ireland and witnessed the destruction left in his wake, including gutted churches, razed villages, and destroyed trades. After marrying her young soldier-husband, she lived through the so-called "Williamite Wars" or "War of the Two Kings" beginning in the 1680s, which resulted in the loss of their grand estate in the west of Ireland. She became a witness to vicious battles and sieges, deaths and deprivations, and, ultimately, was forced into exile in France - a life of woe and turmoil that cast a dark hue over her mood.

Our estate in France was grand enough and seemed to be a fitting replacement for our lost lands in Ireland. The estate was relatively large in size and grew various crops – wheat, barley, hops, but most especially grapes. We produced wine, not in vast quantities, but of select vintages. I watched this labor with great fascination, especially the process of making barrels and casks for the wine. I asked the estate's steward and its workers if I might assist them, and they eagerly accepted my offer of free labor. I became quite an accomplished cooper and winemaker and seriously considered entering the European wine trade. John, on the other hand, seemed to have no outside interests other than religion and politics. He lived on a stipend provided by our father yet spurned his fatherly affection. As we grew older, most of John's time was spent in crowded coffeehouses and taverns, listening to and debating with those who were disloyal to the French crown. It was a dangerous pastime that risked seeing him in irons in a French royal prison. There is no question in my mind that he was closely watched by the king's spies, and had they considered him a real threat of any kind, he would have disappeared.

We spoke no Irish in our household, as Father thought it best that we learn the language of our enemy (the English) and the language of our hosts (the French). A proficient language teacher was engaged for this purpose. I learned a few words of Irish from friends but never became a proficient speaker. Occasionally, Father uttered Irish profanity when he was particularly upset. He also dropped the "O" from our surname, and we simply became the "Finns." He also insisted that John and I both learn Irish history, taught by him personally, but over time, John began to challenge Father's perspective on historical events in Ireland, leading Father to eventually give up this effort in frustration.

As an influential Irish officer who had proven his worth in battle, our father, along with our mother and their children, were expected to attend to the king (now Louis XV) at his palace at Versailles on special occasions. The massive palace was decadent in more ways than one. Many in the French male aristocracy who surrounded the young king wore brilliant white hosiery, some with fur-fringed capes, and all wore cocked hats, coats, waistcoats, and breeches just below the knee, made of required French fabric only. They also donned expensive long wigs and metal badges of distinction. They all sought to gain the king's attention and royal favor, often trying to say or do something amusing or flattering to the king. The women wore elaborate, multi-tiered wigs, heavy makeup, and enormous round silk dresses, gathered tightly at the waist. They, too, sought the king's attention and favor, with some even willing to engage with the monarch if that was what was needed to gain wealth and influence.

Both sexes soaked themselves in gallons of perfume to mask the smell of their unwashed bodies. Guests at Versailles were also in the habit of relieving themselves wherever they pleased in the voluminous palace, despite strategically located chamber pots being made available. This left it to some 9000 palace servants to clean the enormous piles of smelly human waste from those gilded halls each night. There was much gossip, palace intrigue, elaborate balls and feasts that went on for days, shooting and hunting contests, and the swapping of bed partners. Somewhat seduced by this libertine atmosphere, I abandoned my state of chastity for the beautiful daughter of a Marquis who was quick to demonstrate her loose morals (and considerable talents) during one of my visits to the royal palace. My Catholic, conservative parents detested the social and moral atmosphere at Versailles but dared not raise open objections to it that might give offense to their royal benefactor.

John, of course, was horrified by the French displays of kingly power and excess at Versailles. He became more radicalized and rebellious as a result of being exposed to them. To John, Versailles represented everything corrupt and irreligious that was inherent in the Catholic monarchies of Europe. He showed no further interest in adhering to the dictates of our Catholic religion or in joining my father, now serving in France's "Irish Brigade" – a six-regiment elite force of Irish volunteers. John increasingly talked of leaving France for good for some Protestant sanctuary when he had an opportunity to do so. These sentiments riled my father to no end, as he expected his eldest son to follow him into the Franco-Irish military and then inherit the chateau and estate.

I had no objection to serving France in the military, and at the age of 20, I decided to join the Irish Brigade. That was the same year John declared that he was leaving France for Ireland and a new life serving our sworn enemies. Father was, at first, irate and combative, then heartbroken and despondent. He disowned his first-born son. I secretly wished John well as he departed. I bore him no ill will and expressed brotherly affection for him. In other words, "I had his back." But I had never been through the fires of war and suffering that my father and mother had endured during their years of service to the Catholic James II in pursuit of our family's welfare and well-being—and neither had John. I hoped that John was making an informed and rational, not purely emotional, choice to leave France. Neither Mother nor Erin saw John off on his trip to Ireland, as that would have represented one more crushing emotional blow to our father. Erin, however, followed John's future progress through correspondence shared by mutual friends who frequently wrote to him.

Once in the ranks of the Irish Brigade, I found army life to be mostly enjoyable – hard, yet enjoyable. The food and pay were bad, the training was physically taxing, and the discipline was severe. However, I was a quick study of drill and the use of weapons, including muskets, pistols, war rapiers, and the bayonet. I even had an opportunity to pick up some vital cavalry skills, although the Irish Brigade consisted of infantry only. Our Irish regiment wore "Stuart Red" uniforms, and the Irish Brigade forged an unmatched record for valor in the service of the French crown during what came to be known as the War of the Austrian Succession, including the important Battle of Fontenoy in May 1745, where we turned the English right flank, capturing colors and cannons in a memorable triumph. I made a close friend in the Brigade, Sean O'Boyle, and we often went carousing in Paris while on leave. But one drunkenly splendid weekend, our leave was cut short when we received word from our superiors by courier that select men from our regiments – 50 from each of the six Irish regiments - would be sent to Scotland to aid in the Jacobite Rising in 1745. Both O'Boyle and I would be among the selected troops. We knew little of Scotland other than it was cold, close to Ireland, and was a Gaelic brother nation in peril from the English.

The 1745 Rising was sparked by the "Young Pretender," Charles Edward Stuart, the grandson of James II and son of James Edward Stuart, with Charles being popularly known as "Bonnie Prince Charlie." He landed in Scotland with only seven of his closest followers at the time, including the influential Franco-Irish officer John O'Sullivan. He called on the Scottish clans to rebel once more, reject the unpopular 1707 Union of England and Scotland, restore the Stuarts to both the Scottish and English thrones, and await a planned French invasion of Great Britain. The Catholic Highland clans and many non-conforming Protestant clans were keen for a new rising – a new opportunity to reset the political table within the British Isles in favor of the Stuarts or, at the very least, in support of Scottish independence.

One thousand clansmen immediately rallied to Charlie's standard, which was raised at Glenfinnan on August 19, 1745. They marched on and captured Edinburgh on September 17th and then, the very next day, proclaimed James Edward Stuart as King of Scotland, with Charlie as his 'regent' (and thus the 'de facto' king in James's stead). They went on to eventually defeat two British armies sent against them, and with a newly raised 5,000-man force, the Jacobites pushed as far south as Derby in England by year's end. The English throne seemed within reach of the Stuarts, but then things started to go wrong: Few Englishmen would come out to support, let alone join, the Stuarts; supplies dried up as the British Royal Navy blockaded the coasts and seized Jacobite stores in transit; no French invasion force appeared; the Jacobite army risked being trapped between two converging British armies. A retreat to Scotland was decided upon by a divided and fractious Jacobite leadership (the professional French, Irish, and Scottish officers were sometimes at odds with the Scottish clan leaders). A Jacobite siege of Stirling Castle, the acknowledged gateway to the Highlands, was rebuffed, and a new, seasoned British army was coming for them, commanded by the Duke of Cumberland, George II's youngest son (whom we in the Irish Brigade had met and helped to defeat at Fontenoy).

The bickering Jacobite leadership resolved, first and foremost, to protect their supply cache in Inverness, Scotland. However, to their east, outside the village of Culloden, the Jacobite and British armies unexpectedly met on the battlefield. I was present on that fateful day and felt a deep sense of concern, not just for my welfare but because I had learned through Erin's correspondence with her friends that my brother, John, was now serving in the British-Irish army, part of a battalion of troops brought from Ireland to reinforce the Duke of Cumberland's forces and fight against the Jacobites.

The rift within our family now had the potential for deadly consequences as the two armies gathered and prepared to collide.

2. Culloden

We were known as Irish "Picquets," a group of soldiers assigned to a special duty. Our "special duty" was to bolster and assist the Jacobite army in Scotland, which was under pressure from a British army commanded by the Duke of Cumberland. He had arrived in Great Britain with 12,000 veteran troops from the fighting in Flanders. Cumberland also began to reform, rearm, and resupply the British border garrisons that had been defeated and dispersed by charging Scottish clansmen, who let out a bone-chilling 'Highland yell,' at the earlier battles of Prestonpans and Falkirk. Strengthened by an infusion of seasoned troops and new supplies, the once-defeated royal troops were preparing to fight once more. Cumberland not only brought new reinforcements with him but also introduced a new tactic learned on the battlefields of Europe from the Swedes: his troops were instructed to form up three lines of infantry – the first to release a devastating volley of musket fire, then kneel; the second line to do the same, then repeat what the first line had done, with both lines reloading their muskets as they knelt; the third line would then engage, fire the final volley, and begin to reload while the first line stood, ready to fire once more. This cycle would be repeated, delivering a cascade of continuous fire that seemed never-ending. This tactic would have a considerable effect on the fighting to come. Our frontline Scottish clansmen, although exceedingly brave, were unaccustomed to formal battles and were stunned, then torn apart, by this new British tactic that they had not encountered in previous encounters with enemy troops.

At the time of the Battle of Culloden, our Irish picquets consisted of about 300 men, supported by 70 Irish cavalrymen from "Fitzjames Horse," who were largely without their horses, having lost most of them to a seizure by Britain's Royal Navy while being transported by sea. By the end of 1745, only about half of our initially assigned picquets had arrived in Scotland. Brigadier Walter Stapleton commanded our forces, with soldiers from our "Dillon," "Rooth," and "Lally" regiments making it to the battle area by late 1745. They were later supported by troops from the separate "Berwick" regiment in February 1746. "Bonnie Prince Charlie's" forces totaled about 5,000 when the Battle of Culloden was joined on April 16th, 1746. Cumberland's advancing forces numbered some 8,000 British troops assembled in 16 infantry battalions, including four Scottish battalions and one Irish battalion, a testament to the divided loyalties at play in the conflict.

The decision by the Jacobite command to defend their supplies in Inverness ultimately led to Culloden, east of Inverness, being the site of the pivotal battle of the Jacobite Rising, often referred to as the "45." It was not a location greatly loved by any of the Jacobite commanders, but it was considered better than all of the other suggested alternative battlefields, most of which were both considered and rejected.

Cumberland advanced north from his new headquarters at Aberdeen, Scotland, as winter turned to spring in 1746 and then advanced west toward Inverness. While Cumberland had to leave some troops behind to guard against possible Jacobite insurrections and any resulting advances on his rear areas, he was reinforced by new battalions as he made his way up north and west. By April 12th, 1746, Cumberland was ready to cross the Spey River, but he was facing a 2,000-man Jacobite force commanded by Lord John Drummond guarding the potential crossing points. However, Drummond decided that the Jacobite force could not prevent the British crossing and chose to retreat rather than oppose Cumberland, a controversial move. Cumberland crossed the Spey undisturbed and advanced on Nairn, Scotland, which the Jacobite forces also evacuated on April 14th. Given evolving events and the failure to confront Cumberland on the Spey, some Jacobite commanders wanted to abandon Inverness as well. But they faced the question of - where to go and with what resources?

Already short of material, mainly due to the British naval blockade of the Scottish coasts, most of the Jacobite leadership could not bear to leave carefully collected supplies to the British following a hasty retreat from Inverness. John O'Sullivan, the Franco-Irish commander who had initially accompanied Prince Charles to Scotland, identified Drummossie 'Muir' or moor near Culloden on the eastern approaches to Inverness as a place to make a stand if one was to be made at all. It was a flat moor bordered by dikes and stone walls, not an ideal place to fight, but every other suggested location had major drawbacks. Protecting the road to Inverness was crucial, and that fact decided the matter. Every other potential battlefield within easy reach would not fulfill that requirement. The Jacobite army moved east to Culloden, but they arrived at a place different from the exact location initially identified by O'Sullivan. The weather was nasty, the army was confused, and Cumberland's plans were a mystery. Still, the Jacobite leaders had finally resolved to fight.

The fact that the Duke of Cumberland was set to celebrate his 25th birthday may have played a role in determining the outcome of the coming battle. Jacobite forces learned that two gallons of brandy had been distributed to each British regiment in celebration of the Duke's birthday, and they hoped to catch the British troops in a drunken state, simply unaware, or both. Lord George Murray, one of the Jacobite commanders, suggested a night attack on the British camp outside of Nairn, playing to the raiding strengths of the Scottish clansmen. However, things went wrong from the very start. Afraid of being spotted by Royal Navy ships at anchor in the Moray Firth, the Jacobite force waited until the night was pitch black before moving out. With no distinct trail to follow, confusion and disorientation set in, and most of the attackers did not approach the British lines until an hour before dawn. Fearing a daylight attack on a numerically superior force, Jacobite leaders decided to abort the raid. Yet, some of the raiders were still in transit, and some forces even passed one another in the darkness without knowing of each other's presence. Communications were dismal, field orders were contradictory, and the whole Jacobite force finally decided to retire back to where they had started near Culloden, with orders to that effect. However, Cumberland's forces had been alerted to the presence of lead elements of the Jacobite raiders nearby, prompting the British leadership to go after their enemy immediately. Decisive action would ultimately bring advantages on the battlefield.

The morning of April 16th, 1746, was snowy, cold, wet, and uncomfortable. Returning Jacobite troops from the raid on Nairn drifted off to forage for food, fell into roadside ditches, or sought shelter in abandoned shepherd's huts, wrapped in their cloaks for some much-needed sleep. Others headed for Inverness, where they knew supplies and hot food were waiting. Several hundred fighters were thus absent when word spread that Cumberland's forces were quickly advancing on the Jacobite army. Orders went out for what remained of the army to form up and be prepared to meet Cumberland at Drummossie. I asked O'Boyle, my companion since France, "Are you ready for this fight?" He smiled and said, "We have not faced weather quite this bad before, my friend, but we've weathered battles worse than what's to come. We will do just fine." O'Boyle was always the eternal optimist!

Our picquets were accustomed to the type of fighting typically associated with an opponent like Cumberland's army. At the Battle of Fontenoy, for instance, our troops in the Irish Brigade were part of a 60,000-man French army confronting an allied army of about equal size. Culloden, by comparison, would be a small clash: 5,000 men (Jacobite) versus 8,000 men (British). Our troops were positioned in the second Jacobite line on the far-left flank, close to where Prince Charles was located with his commanders, including Lords Drummond, Murray, the Irishman O'Sullivan, and others. The Scottish clansmen would be the first to fight. Their lead elements, consisting of mid-level landowners, were mostly armed with traditional Scottish broadswords, small shields, and pistols. The ranks carried French and Spanish firelocks, but there was a sprinkling of swords, pistols, and even a few farm implements. Our picquets were well-armed with French muskets, but the Jacobite cavalry had few horses, and our meager number of cannons were mainly

3-pounders. The British had more of everything: more troops, more mounted cavalry, more artillery, including 3-pounders and mortars, and more munitions. Their officers carried pistols and swords. Their infantry ranks were completely fitted out with "Brown Bess" .75 caliber muskets, named after a common title for a rather plain-looking whore.

As we finished forming up, Cumberland's forces arrived in front of us around ten in the morning. Our side put on a brave face, cheering and hurling insults at our opponents, especially the Scots, who excelled at that activity. The British said nothing in reply, simply advancing until they were about 600 yards away. Both sides shuffled their units to gain some tactical advantage, but it seemed to have little effect. The British brought up their artillery, and a brief exchange of cannon fire took place around one in the afternoon, inflicting light casualties on both sides. It was then time for one side or the other to make a move, but Cumberland would not oblige us. Our leaders decided to advance first. The weather had finally turned fair, the moor was soggy but passable, and the clansmen were excited and ready to be sent forward. However, when it came time to go, some Scottish formations balked and argued with our leadership, as they had not been assigned the 'lead' position in the advance—a matter of honor and Highland battlefield etiquette. It seemed that the issue was finally negotiated and resolved, and the advance recommenced in earnest. It was hoped that the Scots would shock the British ranks with their ferocity and force them to take to their heels, as in previous encounters. It was not to be.

First, "grapeshot" and similarly deadly "canister shot" were fired by the British artillery, sowing havoc among the advancing Scottish ranks. Squeezed between low stone walls on either flank, the Scots weathered the artillery storm much as they had weathered the snow and freezing rainstorm in the early morning, but with considerable, ugly casualties. Their advance was jagged, slowed by the soggy ground. Then, when the Scottish lead elements were just twelve yards out, the three rows of British infantry unleashed their deadly, consecutive waves of thunderous musket fire. Most clansmen were brought down with multiple wounds well before they ever reached the British lines. Yet, miraculously, some staggered into Cumberland's ranks, swinging their swords until British musket balls or bayonets punctured their necks, lungs, or other vital organs. Out of sheer frustration at being unable to reach the British lines in the hail of musket fire, some Scots even resorted to throwing stones at their enemies until they, too, were cut down. The famous "Highland charge" was irretrievably broken. The Scottish line staggered, stopped, and then mostly fell back.

As I stood looking at the carnage unfolding before me, I hopelessly scanned the battlefield through the black powder smoke and crush of men, searching for a glimpse of my brother's face. It was an impossible task, of course, picking out one man in a sea of combatants amidst the sheer anarchy of it all. Our picquets finally received their orders from our officers: "Pret! Portez! Armez!" (Ready, Carry, Load), and finally, "En avant!" (Forward). "Ready to go, brother?" O'Boyle asked, but I never answered. We marched straight into the hell of battle, attempting to steady our collapsing front ranks, but ultimately to no avail. British dragoons pursued the now fleeing Jacobite right flank and smashed into our lines as well. We stood firm, however, hoping that our retreating front ranks could somehow flow through us and then reform at our back, but it was not possible. An unnerving rout had set in among the troops. We lost one-quarter to one-half of our contingent while valiantly holding our ground, acting as a rear guard. O'Boyle and I emerged unscathed from the clash of arms, but Jacobite casualties were horrific: severed limbs, severed heads, men shot to pieces by 'grapeshot,' men shot to pieces by condensed musket fire, men 'speared' in all manner of places on their bodies by swords and bayonets. The wounded on the ground wriggled in intense pain, cried out in delirium for their mothers to come and comfort them, and moaned an unnerving moan. Our Irish troops were finally surrounded by dragoons and were facing advancing British infantry with fixed bayonets. Only when we had finally secured an escape route for the Jacobite leaders and ranks, including Prince Charles and many clansmen fleeing from the battlefield, did we lay down our arms. I later heard that "Bonnie Prince Charlie" declared that he wished he had died on the field at Culloden.

Despite its savagery, the whole battle had only lasted an hour.

Our Jacobite army suffered some 2,000 casualties, while the British had lost a mere 50 dead and about 250 wounded. Early on, our British captors assured us that, being regular French troops, we would not be harmed but eventually traded for British troops captured on the continent by the French. This was not the case for many Irish or French 'volunteers,' Scottish clan leaders, or British deserters, most of whom were executed without trial or any other form of consideration. In fact, the retreating Jacobite clansmen, even their wounded on the field of battle, were given "no quarter" by order of the British commanders and were run to the ground and slaughtered without an opportunity to surrender.

We French troops were locked up for a time in a Scottish fort, then marched south and finally transferred to a prison barge on the Thames. The food on the barge was hardly edible, and we were mostly kept in chains or forced to work at hard labor. It was not uncommon for unruly prisoners to be disciplined with the lash or, in cases of inciting a riot or murder, to be hanged. Luckily, we only spent about five months on the barge before a prisoner exchange was arranged between the warring armies. O'Boyle, who had accompanied me into captivity, and I were finally returned to French soil. Our Scottish war was over.

3. Return and Repatriation

CALAIS, FRANCE, 28TH OF OCTOBER, 1746.

"Father is dead," Erin declared, her voice carrying the weight of grief. "Dead and buried." The news shocked me, abruptly pulling me from the state of joy I felt at being returned to France as part of a prisoner-of-war exchange. I had not seen my sister since the summer of 1745, and it pained me to witness the look of sorrow etched across her face. Erin went on to explain that Father had not succumbed to old age or disease but had fallen victim to an exploding enemy mortar bomb while conferring with French and Irish officers on the battlefield. He had died fighting for the Catholic monarchs and the Irish cause that had consumed most of his adult life. While I considered him my hero, I knew that my wayward brother, John, considered him a deluded fool.

Erin had come to meet me, ready to assist in transporting me and my few belongings by carriage back to our chateau, with my parole allowing me this extended leave. The French military had informed my family of the date and location of my release from British captivity. I was well aware that I would have to rejoin the Irish Brigade later but released prisoners received an initial reprieve. I said my goodbyes to O'Boyle, assuring him that we would meet again in the ranks of the French army. He bade me farewell for now, but not goodbye. I was headed to see my mother and to handle our affairs in the wake of Father's passing, including arrangements for the future of our estate, which Father had bequeathed to me alone in his will. John received nothing from Father except his utter contempt. Erin and Mother were now in my care, as they could not legally inherit property, but they did receive stipends from Father, which I managed on their behalf for their living expenses.

My years in the army had left me restless. I harbored no desire to oversee the day-to-day running of an estate. Fortunately, our estate functioned rather smoothly, primarily managed by our capable steward, Monsieur Rousseau, along with our laborers and servants. Mother and my sister were also involved in the estate's management, as Father was often away with the army. I saw no reason to disrupt this established arrangement, as I, too, remained in the army. I secured an allowance for myself in Louis d'or Coin and established a trust, overseen by a local avocat, to manage the estate's affairs and support my mother and sister.

However, I did harbor a desire to visit Ireland at some point—a near-mythical land I had never actually seen but had fought for in the name of. I yearned to reunite with John and attempt to reconcile with him. Mutual friends had identified John as a survivor of Culloden and subsequent British occupation duties in Scotland. They mentioned that he was somewhere back in Ireland with the army, possibly in Cork City or Killarney, in the Kerry region of southwestern Ireland. I was determined to find him once my military service was at an end, believing that the bond we had forged in our youth would endure whatever political or religious disagreements we might encounter.

By 1748, the clouds of war in Europe had finally dissipated, bringing peace to the world once more. As a result of the Treaty of Aix-la-Chapelle in October 1748, the European combatants had concluded their nearly worldwide conflict. O'Boyle and I were mustered out of the Irish Brigade as France downsized its enormous armies. France, while still a formidable continental military power, had gained little but resentment against Great Britain from the war. Many viewed the new peace as a temporary respite from fighting, rather than a permanent solution. France's navy could not match the British fleet and suffered significant losses in naval encounters. Moreover, the war had drained the French royal treasury.

Under the terms of the 1748 peace, France was forced to withdraw from parts of the Netherlands and gained little in America, aside from the return of a strategically important colonial fortress lost to the British during the conflict.

For the Jacobites, the war and its aftermath were unmitigated disasters. Charles Edward Stuart barely escaped Scotland with his life after Culloden, leaving behind a trail of devastation, defeat, and British retaliation. His followers were displaced, dispersed, and, in many cases, executed. His promise of a French invasion of England had remained unfulfilled. Though still hailed as a champion by some Jacobites, the French had, by treaty, ceased their support for the Jacobite cause and any Stuart claims to the English throne. In a surprising turn of events, the French even arrested and expelled Prince Charles from France. He was taken into custody during a surprise incident at the Paris Opera and was subsequently jailed for a time. "Bonnie Prince Charlie" was then exiled to live in a Papal enclave in the south of France, where he descended into drink, despair, and debauchery, and even contemplated converting to Protestantism if it could somehow help him gain the British throne. Alas, it would not.

Betrayed by their adopted nation, France, and their own prince, Charles Edward Stuart, many exiled Irish Jacobites retained their hatred for the British occupiers of Ireland. They clung to their Catholic faith and transformed their hatred and faith into an ardent desire for Irish liberation from Great Britain through means other than the Stuart dynasty. I had become one of those lost and abandoned Irishmen, and my unwavering goal was to return to the land of my forefathers, find my brother, and somehow strike back against our oppressors, if possible. Before leaving the army, I asked Sean O'Boyle if he had ever considered traveling to Ireland. He replied, "I do not know what kind of reception I would receive once I got there, but I would be prepared to risk it." We made plans to go together and seek our fortunes. Now, I had to break the news to Mother and Erin.

Upon my return to the chateau, I summoned my mother and sister to join me in our library, where I intended to reveal my impending departure. As we faced each other, I struggled to find the right words, knowing that my announcement might not be well received.

"I plan to go live in Ireland," I blurted out abruptly. "I've made provisions for both of you to continue living comfortably here on the estate. If you ever need anything, I'll share my location in that country so you can write to me."

"You are mad," Mother exclaimed, her face turning ashen gray. "I suppose you also plan to seek out your heretic brother while you are there. You two are well-matched in abandoning your family. Nothing good will come of your absence, for you or for us. Misery and death await you in that country," she declared, her words sounding chillingly cold and prophetic.

"You are both secure here. I will give you the particulars of the arrangements I have made for you and introduce you to the local avocat responsible for your care. As for me, I have learned to fend for myself while in the army. I am committed to this course of action because the place where you and Father were born calls to me," I explained.

"You are misguided," Mother countered. "Ireland is not what it was when I was a girl growing up there, and I am sure it is not what you think it is today. Our Catholic earls and armies have been driven off the island, and Protestant oppression has only grown more extreme. Poverty and want rule the countryside. You will be suspect from the minute you arrive there, and I fear you may never see me alive again once you leave. I am glad that you believe you can fend for yourself, all while forgoing your responsibilities to this family. Your father would be aghast at your choice. I can only bid you a not-so-fond farewell."

Mother then stood up and swiftly departed the room, leaving me with a sense of finality. In the days that followed, I saw her only infrequently. She refused to speak to me or even make eye contact, making it clear that she was violently upset with my decision to go to Ireland.

Erin, on the other hand, was constantly in tears due to our family feud and my imminent departure. She had already lost John to Ireland, and now I was leaving as well. The responsibility for managing the estate and Mother's affairs would now fall on her shoulders. I knew that my sister was entertaining a suitor, a Mister O'Malley of the Franco-Irish gentry, whom I had met only once. He was moderately wealthy, moved in the same social circles as Erin, and I could see her getting married soon. Financial security was assured for her, as I had made certain of it, and provisions were in place.

However, Mother's situation was different. She would be financially secure but not emotionally content. "You will have to be the support for our mother now, Erin, her rock," I advised.

Erin replied, "I appreciate the forces that compel you to go, but I have to agree with Mother that this move to Ireland is a fool's errand."

I packed only my haversack for the journey and made my rounds on the estate to bid farewell to those laborers and servants I had grown up with, some of whom had become dear friends. Several of our female servants were more than just acquaintances. Erin hugged me in the portico of the chateau, wishing me the best and urging me to seek out our mother before I left. However, I chose not to do so, deciding to spare Mother further unhappiness.

Now it was off to reunite with O'Boyle, whom I had contacted by post, and to secure passage for both of us on a French ship departing from Calais, bound for the port of Cork in Ireland's southeast.

Cork had once again become France's gateway to Ireland now that peace was restored, but I had learned from various Irish exiles that trade with Ireland was heavily restricted. British ports and goods were now strongly favored, and the British made it difficult for non-smuggled goods to enter Ireland. Both the British and Irish parliaments worked to undermine many Irish industries in favor of English products and producers. Wool production was especially hard hit, and other Irish products like cattle, beer, cotton, silk, gunpowder, and iron were gradually restricted. Entire

Irish trades collapsed, leaving the population dependent primarily on the land for sustenance.

However, the rich thrived much better than the poor, as the English had confiscated most of the best agricultural and grazing lands in Ireland. The Irish poor survived primarily on a diet of potatoes and milk, with occasional fish and game, although hunting deer had been forbidden by law since Norman times. In contrast, the Protestant estate owners feasted on mutton, pork, beef, vegetables, fish, and game. The Protestant gentry in the towns enjoyed an even wider variety of foods, some imported from Europe. Bakeries and public houses filled the urban areas. The Catholic urban poor, many of whom were ejected from their traditional trades, struggled to survive in poverty and squalor under constant suspicion.

As a result, Ireland was always simmering with a rebellious spirit just below the surface of civil society.

The personal risks to both O'Boyle and me were considerable as we returned to the island. Catholics who had served in the French military were immediately under suspicion, and many Jacobite families and individuals had been officially outlawed and banned by the government from ever returning to Ireland, given the terms of their enforced absence. Should they suddenly appear, they would be sought out for arrest and imprisonment. Not really knowing our own legal status, O'Boyle and I would have to tread softly once we were in the country.

Cork sat on an island in one of the largest natural harbors in the world. The port began as a Norse trading center and was still a trader's dream location. It was known in Ireland and Great Britain as a "rebel city," like various other towns and cities in the south of the country that had frequently fought on the losing side of the religious and ethnic wars that had swept across Ireland during the last five centuries. Cork had been captured by Cromwell and later besieged and ultimately captured by John Churchill, William of Orange's chief general. Not only did French traders, especially those involved in the wine trade, make Cork their base of operations once the peace was reinstated, but fleeing French Protestants also made this old Catholic bastion their new home.

Upon landing in Cork, O'Boyle and I avoided the authorities, found lodging near the cattle market, and, of course, set out to find a good public house. A thatched-roof drinking establishment called "The Market Stall" was found, and for several nights, O'Boyle and I drank beer and whiskey in that place. Suddenly, one night, a man rose from his seat and started reciting a Jacobite poem, "Ode on the Battle of Gladsmuir," about the Jacobite victory over British forces at Prestonpans in 1745. A group of British soldiers drinking in the place took offense to the poem, and a fight erupted. Fists, chairs, tankards, and jars were thrown during the melee. One patron stood on a table and yelled, "Faugh a Ballagh" ("Clear the way" in Irish), apparently a traditional Irish battle cry. This action escalated the fighting until local "watchmen" or constables and a platoon of British soldiers arrived on the scene and broke up the fighting. They beat some patrons worse than they had experienced in the initial fight. O'Boyle and I managed to slip out the back of the public house after the forces of law and order arrived. The fight was our introduction to just how raw political sensibilities in Ireland could be.

The next day, I summoned up the courage to inquire at the local British Army garrison about whether my brother John might be serving among them. "No. No 'John Finn' here among our ranks. He must be stationed elsewhere," a gruff sergeant maintained. "The regiments move about to where they are most needed. He may even be in America or Gibraltar. Come back in a few months, and he may be here by then," the sergeant said. Then he looked at me slyly, saying, "Have you ever been in the army?" He may have suspected I was an army deserter. "No, no," I said, "I am a lover, not a fighter." He chuckled and bid me farewell. My search for my brother would go on. Another day, another garrison.

One day, while walking near the remnants of Cork's old town walls, I spotted a broadside advertising a need for coopers in Killarney. I knew the trade and thought it was a good opportunity. O'Boyle and I had no strong connection to Cork, and he hailed from a West Country family as well. We were both without work, and O'Boyle especially needed a means of sustenance. After some consideration, we decided to each buy a horse, gather our belongings, and make our way to Killarney, in County Kerry, which had held its designation as a county since Norman times.

I purchased a black stallion, which I named "Mercury," while O'Boyle secured a chestnut mount.

The 18-league journey from Cork to Killarney was said to be fraught with danger, plagued by both political bandits and those solely driven by greed. To protect ourselves, I acquired a thrusting knife. With our preparations complete, we set off westward towards County Kerry. The journey, however, proved to be uneventful, and we finally arrived in the mountainous southwest.

4. Killarney

KILLARNEY, KERRY, 6TH OF MAY, 1750.

The "Penal Laws" were a series of legal disabilities imposed on Catholics and non-conforming Protestant sects in Ireland by the Irish Parliament, which was dominated by the Church of Ireland's "Protestant Ascendancy" — a popular term for the clique that controlled Irish affairs. These laws were specifically designed to keep Irish populations in a state of subjugation. While some "Penal Laws" were in place during the 1600s, complete Protestant control over the entire island was not assured at the time. However, everything changed in 1691 with the removal of large Catholic military forces from Ireland. It was then that the authorities decided to put potential rebels under Dublin's (and London's) boot. These "Penal Laws" transformed all individuals, except those adhering to the state-supported Protestant Church of Ireland (Ireland's Protestant equivalent to the Church of England), into "second" or even "third" class citizens of the Crown of Great Britain and Ireland.

Here are some examples of what Catholics were prohibited from doing after 1691:

Catholics were excluded from holding public office and could not sit in the Irish Parliament.

Catholics could not marry Protestants.

Catholics could not own firearms (a prohibition I would soon violate) or serve in the military.

Catholics could not join the legal profession.

Catholics could not attend Trinity College, Dublin.

Catholics could not inherit Protestant land.

Catholics could not own a horse of a value exceeding five pounds (a prohibition I had already violated).

Catholics could not teach school or instruct their youth.

These and other prohibitions, related to property and behavior, were enforced rigorously, liberally, or sometimes not at all, depending on where you resided in Ireland. Killarney, being considered, like Cork, a "rebel city," found itself under rigorous enforcement. Regardless of the varying degrees of oppression, two facts stood out prominently: first, the 90% Catholic population of Ireland had no say in their own governance, and second, that 90% of the population now only owned about 10% of the land in Ireland. The "Penal Laws" helped to support this wholesale disenfranchisement of the Irish.

I found Kerry to be a wildly beautiful region in Ireland's southwest. With access to the ocean, it had long been open to French and Spanish trade, influences, and political intrigue. Always rebellious, the region had witnessed major death and destruction during the so-called "Desmond Rebellions" (1569 - 1583), and later, the near-destruction of the O'Sullivan clan during O'Sullivan's "Beare" or Chief's epic march from south to north in 1602, when the English and their allies massacred close to 1000 members of that family. What followed was the mass confiscation of both castles and estates in western Ireland by Elizabeth I's Tudor invaders in the wake of the Nine Years War (1593-1603). However, it was a region where the Irish language was still strong and where our traditional music, poetry, and beliefs survived and thrived. Killarney ('Cill Airne' in Irish) was situated on the shores of Lough Leane and was surrounded by a land of lakes and very fair mountains. It was close to the site of a famous abbey dating from the 600s, which educated early kings and councilors of Ireland. As with so many towns in Ireland, Killarney was ravaged by Cromwellian forces in the 1650s.

O'Boyle found lodging in the town's center, but I traveled to its western fringes, where I came upon the "Black Horse Inn." I thought that the place represented a good omen, as I had just purchased a black horse! The inn offered stables and care for visitors' horses, good food and drink served on the lower level, and suitable, reasonably priced sleeping chambers above. One of the best attractions of the place was its server and barmaid, Ginny O'Neill, a red-haired beauty with a quick wit and a generous bosom. She knew how to catch the attention of the inn's male patrons and occasionally disappeared with the wealthier customers for some private entertainment. She was someone I hoped to get to know much better.

The inn was owned and managed by one Brendan O'Conner, who obviously had some arrangement to share in any profits accumulated by his lovely barmaid. He was a large and boisterous fellow, well-suited to running a roadhouse. He took no nonsense from unruly patrons, personally tossing out those causing any form of disturbance. I paid for a small chamber a month in advance and set about seeing if I could catch the attention of Miss O'Neill (whom I assumed was unmarried — a fact later confirmed by O'Connor). Unfortunately, she paid me no mind but showered her attention on the well-dressed gentry. However, I was not discouraged. My time would come.

The next day, I made my way to "McCarthy and Sons," the coopers who had posted the broadside seeking workers from Cork. I convinced old McCarthy that I knew the trade well enough to be of assistance to him, and he took me on, as he was short of workers. My tasks mainly involved two things: first, making casks, barrels, buckets, and similar items from heated wooden staves, bound together with metal hoops; second, hitching up a donkey cart to transport the finished cooperage around Killarney and to Cork based on customer orders. Some cooperage was destined for brewers or public houses, while others were for ships to carry water and provisions. Wine and spirit makers also bought our products. Most sales trips to Cork were uneventful, but every so often, I was stopped by "highwaymen" on the route — who soon let me go when they found out I carried no money. These robbers were not after barrels and casks; some were very gentlemanly and firm, yet respectful, while others were brutish louts who would knock you from your cart if no money was to be found. I found the first group impressive — they dressed well, rarely resorted to violence, and had a spirit of liberty and a 'devil-may-care' attitude that was appealing. Regardless of the type of robber one might encounter, however, you had to be cautious on the return trip to Killarney, as that's when you carried the proceeds from the Cork sales. I soon learned that you were less likely to encounter a highwayman around dinner hour when most of them were otherwise engaged.

"Why do you not show me more attention?" I asked Ginny the barmaid one evening while I was having a jar of whiskey at the inn. She laughed and said, "You cannot afford me. I know you are a cooper, and no barrel maker can feed my tastes." I replied, "You are sadly mistaken. I am a French aristocrat. Your tastes are not beyond my means." She challenged me, saying, "Speak to me in French then," laughing in disbelief. I then said, "Comment es-tu devenue si belle?" (How did you come to be so beautiful?). She responded with, "Noooooo. You bad bugger. You made that up." I assured her, "No, I did not. Ask anyone who is French what the phrase means." She walked away, laughing even more. I felt that I was making an impression on her. I began buying her jars of whiskey, her favorite drink, every now and then while I was sitting downstairs at the inn. She started to come around, to sit and talk with me at my table, initially only briefly, but then more and more often as time went by.

The whiskey we drank out of Potter's jars was simple "poitin," the illicit type, and not "Parliament whiskey" or the licensed brands distilled by a select group of gentry or peers awarded the 'right' to distill whiskey by the government. Still, the homemade variety was considered the "water of life" by the Irish and a popular spirit.

I once asked Ginny where she was from. She said, "Up North. Our Clan O'Neill used to rule over Ulster and was the most powerful family in all of Ireland. Now these English and Scottish Protestant invaders have reduced us to mere paupers in our own land. I had to come south to find work." I then changed the subject and said, "When are you and I going to go upstairs and get to know one another much better?" She laughed loudly, as usual, and jokingly replied, "I will attend at your bed chamber when you bring me some gold and jewels befitting the Ulster Queen that I am." With a playful demeanor, she then returned to serving beer and whiskey to her admiring male patrons.

One night at the inn, I noticed a gentleman 'holding court' at a corner table, with visitors coming and going, whispering in low voices. I saw him talking with Ginny, and she later came over to see me. She said, "That fellow in the cocked hat in the corner is a Frenchman. Go over and say to him what you previously said to me." I agreed and spoke to him in French. He indicated to Ginny the meaning of the compliment I had paid to her earlier. "Maybe you are a French aristocrat after all," Ginny teased. Her face lit up, she smiled, and then she walked away.

The Frenchman introduced himself as Jacques Boyer, a resident of Brest, France, who spoke good English. We began to converse, and he remarked, "You speak excellent French for an Irishman." I explained that I grew up in Saint-André and had served in the French military at Fontenoy and later at Culloden. "The Irish Brigade, then," Boyer acknowledged. He continued, "I served in the Brigade Normandie during the late war and was at Fontenoy as well. It was a bloody clash for sure, but still a great victory for the French Crown. Some of my closest friends died there."

I suggested that we continue our conversation in French to ensure privacy. Boyer agreed, and we spoke in French about various topics. As we became more comfortable with each other and the whiskey flowed freely, I finally summoned the courage to ask him if he could secure firearms and other weapons for me. Boyer expressed concern that providing firearms to a Catholic like me would violate the country's laws, to which I replied, "Are you in a trade or of a disposition where British or Irish law really makes much of a difference to you?" He laughed and agreed to help, asking about my specific needs and the price I was willing to pay. After discussing the details, we reached an agreement, and I paid him half the purchase price in advance as a sign of our agreement.

However, a month and a half passed with no sign of Boyer. I began to worry that I had been betrayed and that British soldiers might come looking for me. But two months after our initial meeting, Ginny approached me at McCarthy's and informed me that the French trader had returned to the inn and was looking for me. She indicated that he would be at the "Black Horse" that evening.

As soon as my workday ended, I rushed back to the inn, and there sat Boyer at his usual corner table. "Bonjour, Monsieur Finn. I have your tools," the Frenchman said. We decided to retire to my chamber to inspect the merchandise. Boyer fetched the goods while I went upstairs. About twenty minutes later, there was a knock on my door. Boyer had secured exactly what I needed – four new "allary" pistols, two rapiers of the finest French steel, and one cavalry carbine. He also brought powder and shot for the firearms. I was amazed; it was exactly as promised. I paid Boyer the balance owed, and we spent the night drinking whiskey on the main floor of the inn at my expense, served by the lovely Ginny O'Neill.

"Anytime you wish to do business, come and see me here every two months or so. I am a frequent visitor in furtherance of my business pursuits. I know I was late on this last occasion, but it could not be helped in order to properly secure, conceal, and transport your products," Boyer said.

"I have no complaints. Doing business with you has been a distinct pleasure," I replied. But now that I had these instruments of war, what would I do with them?

I had not fully decided to take up the outlaw life. There was still much to consider. Yet, how else would I get Ginny her gold and jewels fit for an Ulster Queen? I had no intention of using my own funds to purchase them. Why not use someone else's money and strike a blow for Irish liberty at the same time? The life of a "Rapparee" beckoned me to take to the highways of Ireland. Maybe O'Boyle would come along with me.

And my search for John continued. I went to the local British garrison in Killarney but was told that no "John Finn" was stationed there. Had he left the army entirely? I would have to resort to the post to explore with Erin and those who knew all of us where he might be located. But the post was slow, and by the time you sent or received letters with information about someone, they may well have disappeared once again to 'God-knows-where.'

I began to think, "Do I really want to find John?" Here I was considering a career as a rebel-leaning highwayman, and John, if he was still in the army, was charged with hunting down rebels. Was a brotherly reunion coming, or some form of violent clash? Only by finding him would the truth be revealed.

5. Rapparee

KILLARNEY, KERRY, 3RD OF SEPTEMBER, 1750.

I was Catholic. It was my tribe, my heritage; but as time passed, "Catholic" became less about my religion and more about my politics. I looked around at the displacement of our Irish people and the resulting poverty and oppression in Ireland and asked, "How could God allow the faithful to suffer so immeasurably?" and "Where was God at the Boyne, at the last siege of Limerick, when Cromwell slaughtered our people by the bushel, or at Fortenoy or Culloden?" How was it that such a faithful servant as my father was permitted to be blown to bits by a heretic enemy's bomb? Difficult questions. No clear answers. I sought those answers less and less in the Mass and the confessional and more in the pursuit of vengeance.

A thirst for vengeance was not hard to come by in Ireland: Irish kings and aristocrats had slaughtered one another, and the Norse, in battles for control over this or that province, but the numbers were relatively small. Then the Normans invaded from England in the 1100s, built their massive stone castles (including Dublin Castle, their longtime stronghold and seat of power), slaughtered hundreds, but eventually ended up wholly dominating only the "Pale" – a strip of land along the east coast of Ireland centered on Dublin. The Tudor English continued to expand the areas of their control and influence, murdering suspected opponents and rebels and confiscating land as they went. Then along came Oliver Cromwell, leader of England's Parliamentary Civil War forces, who had a special hatred for rebellious Irish Catholics. He ravaged the island following a successful Irish revolt in 1641, killing 600,000 or more Irish through battle, massacre, famine, and disease, burned our ancient churches, abbeys, and monasteries, and in 1649 slaughtered the defenders of Drogheda, murdering 2,000 residents - some by burning them alive after many had already surrendered. Wexford, along with other Irish ports, was also sacked, and neither woman nor child were spared by the rampaging Cromwell or his generals. William of Orange, too, killed hundreds of Irish and forced thousands more to flee Ireland for the continent. Both Cromwell and later William 'confiscated' the Catholic Irish right off the best agricultural lands in Ireland, replacing them with English, Scottish, and Irish Protestant "planters." Yes, the Catholic Irish sought vengeance - and with good reason, I would say.

Now that Monsieur Boyer had delivered to me the instruments for my personal vengeance, I sought out Sean O'Boyle, whom I had not seen in some time. He was employed at "Doolin's Iron Works" in Killarney where he was a common laborer. He had time to go out with me for a drink, and over our stubby pint containers of beer, I asked him, "Are you happy with your work?" He looked at me strangely and replied, "If you mean, 'Does it put bread on my table,' then the answer is yes, but it's not a profession that makes my heart race." I then said, "Would you like to be involved with something that will make your heart race?" He leaned in and asked me in a low voice to better explain my proposal. I whispered, "I have secured pistols, powder, shot, two rapiers, and a carbine for you and me to go roving from Kerry to Cork, making the English shite themselves and getting rich at the same time. If you are game, we will occasionally transform ourselves into 'Rapparee' highwaymen and ravage the countryside." O'Boyle's eyes shone bright. "I am certainly game for it. What exactly do you have planned?" He asked. "I was thinking of first raiding a manor house during one of their frequent celebrations and then robbing both the owners and their guests of their money and possessions. I have even seen an inviting target near the lakes, just off the road to Cork. We must be bold; timidity will get us both killed, but I doubt it will be necessary to dispatch anyone if we shock the breeches off them," I said. O'Boyle hungrily devoured every aspect of my plan and agreed to go with me to survey the place in advance of our raid. This would be our first introduction to the profession of the "highwaymen," but we were in no rush. We would plan our assault to the last detail.

There were several contemporary highwaymen operating in Ireland around the time we were preparing to join their ranks. There was James Freny, who hailed from Kilkenny and became famous by riding and raiding with the renowned "Reddy" gang of highway robbers. However, he surrendered in 1749 and ended up betraying his fellows. Then there was Seamus McMurphy from Armagh, who came from a well-known Jacobite family. While roving on the highways and byways, he would stop his victims and announce, "My name is Seamus McMurphy, the most handsome man in Ireland" – quite a vain rogue! Ultimately betrayed by his confederates and rendered drunk, then captured, he was hanged outside his prison for three days in 1750. These were not exactly stories of triumph and glory. O'Boyle and I convinced ourselves that we could do a much better job of it. No ropes for us.

The place we planned to raid was the confiscated estate of a Catholic Irish Earl, now held by a Protestant and former Irish parliamentarian, Mister Taggert. It was known as "Pairceanna Glasa," or "Green Fields," and was a sprawling estate. O'Boyle and I determined from close observations, some through a military glass I had kept since the war, that the footmen at the manor were not armed. The house was close enough to the main road for a rapid escape but was also secluded by large trees. We learned when the next seasonal ball at the manor would be held, masked our faces, brought sacks for our involuntary "collection," and hid our horses in the brush close to the avenue leading to the place.

While a 'minuet' played for the 40 or more guests and the tables were piled high with meats, cheeses, and wines (that our common Irish people could never hope to see, collect, or afford), my partner and I burst through the front doors. I had a pair of French pistols and a rapier, and O'Boyle had a carbine. I yelled, "Turn out your pockets and your purses, for we are the free Irish, and we plan to relieve you of the sweat you have wrung from the people of our island." Our shocking appearance had its effect, and no one raised a hand against us – until one ancient footman decided to play the hero and appeared from the rear of the manor with a loaded musket. I noted his age and resolved to fire into the ceiling of the place with one of my pistols rather than shooting him dead. The discharge was enough for the old gentleman to drop his weapon. I secured the flintlock and collected our winnings from the terrified guests while O'Boyle stood watch. Greatly enriched with gold, rings of every description, ladies' jewels, candlesticks, and silverware, we departed the manor and rode off into the cloudy, stark blackness of a Kerry night.

The robbery greatly alarmed the Protestant establishment throughout Kerry. No one could recall a manor house ever having been invaded before. It was a blow to the 'ascendancy': Protestant landowners were shaken, and the common Irish people took notice of – and celebrated – the raid. The road to Cork was filled with dragoons hunting for the culprits and a hefty reward of 100 pounds was posted on broadsides put up by the authorities for information leading to the capture of the robbers. Soon, those postings were marked over with slogans such as "Saorfaidh Muid Éirinn" ("We will free Ireland" in English), demonstrating popular support for our actions. Meanwhile, O'Boyle and I continued with our ordinary daily pursuits, drawing no suspicion. I split the spoils from the robbery with O'Boyle in an equal fashion, minus the costs of the pistols, rapier, and carbine I provided to him, which we agreed upon in advance.

Monsieur Boyer proved to be a convenient outlet for the products of our robberies. He paid both O'Boyle and me handsomely for the stolen goods we accumulated at the manor house and converted our gold into pounds sterling. When I secured enough ill-gotten money, I resolved to go and speak with Ginny. One fall night, when the inn was especially crowded and the smell of burning turf from the fireplace filled the air, I asked Ginny to come over and chat with me when she had a chance. When a patron stood up to sing an especially stirring rebel song, and the place went quiet, Ginny came to see me at my table. I plunked down a bag of coins and whispered to her, "Is this the price of your attendance at my bedchamber?" She smiled, counted out the coins, and said, "This will suffice – but I know that you can do much better." The devil takes the woman! This beauty was smart and wily, and nothing was ever easy with her. I said, "I can do better." She replied, "That is what they all say." She then said, "I will come to your bedchamber when my work here is done. It could be a while. We are quite busy tonight." I said, somewhat sarcastically, "I await you, my darling, with bated breath."

Around two in the morning, I got a knock on the door. I answered, and it was Ginny, ready for our rendezvous. We quickly undressed and engaged in passionate intimacy like wild animals, against the wall, on the floor, and in my bed. We each then drifted off to sleep, but then I heard her rise early in the morning to dress. "Where are you going?" I asked. She replied, "I have things to do. I am no cooper with set hours." I replied, "Aristocrat, remember?" She laughed, "Oh, yes, aristocrat." I asked, "When will you be back?" She said, "That was enjoyable. We will have to do it again when you can get sufficient funds, Mister Aristocrat." I then inquired, "What would it take to make our little arrangement, let us say, 'exclusive' - you and I forsaking all others?" She winked and said, "A lot more pounds and many gifts, but you can do it, my love. I have genuine faith in you." Cheeky.

As soon as the attention died down over our raid on the manor house, O'Boyle and I set about robbing travelers on the roads fanning out from Killarney: carriages, coaches, supply wagons, and even foot traffic fell victim to our thievery. Sometimes we acted together, sometimes apart. I tried to be prudent while spending my proceeds of crime, but O'Boyle went wild. He quit his trade at the ironworks and became a full-time rogue. He started to draw suspicion onto himself, and it worried me. I did not need more attention from the authorities, nor did O'Boyle.

Two events then shook my personal life: a very late letter arrived from my sister, Erin (who had my return address at the inn), indicating that Mother had died some months ago, and she, Erin, was now married to a Mister O'Malley (just as I had predicted). She indicated that she was 'content' (not happy?) and there was no reason for me to risk a return visit to France to deal with Mother's affairs or in order to congratulate the newly married couple. She noted that Mother had called out for me on her deathbed, then gasped and expired. She then revealed the second earth-shaking event in my life. She knew where John had gotten to after talking with mutual friends. He had been transferred to the 40th Regiment of Foot in Nova Scotia, a British colony in America, where he was involved in skirmishing with French rebels and the Indian people of that place. The news angered me. How many more Irishmen would be sent off fighting England's wars abroad while the Irish at home lived under such a cruel and oppressive system? It did not seem right, and it made me wonder, would I ever see my older brother alive again? I sent Erin 1000 pounds as a wedding gift by way of a draft on my French bank, hoping that she was now on her way to a secure and pleasurable life.

While I continued to take "rewards" home to Ginny from this or that robbery or theft, she still resisted my request for an exclusive relationship. I suppose she asked herself, "Why limit my earning potential?" In turn, I only made available to her sufficient, but not overly generous, proceeds of my crimes to add fuel to her passion. We continued to meet. We drank jars of whiskey together at my table on the ground floor of the inn, and we drank whiskey in my chamber as well, where I kept jars of the stuff. We also engaged in passionate intimacy on a number of occasions.

O'Boyle, too, went wild, engaging in lone, risky highway robberies followed by lavish spending in the local public houses and bragging to a collection of female companions about his heroic exploits on the roads of Ireland. Sheriffs began to hear rumors, grew suspicious, and collaborated on shadowing O'Boyle's movements. When they were certain he was preparing to engage in roadside thievery once again, a coach full of armed men, pretending to be simple gentlemen travelers, set out for O'Boyle's favorite hunting grounds between Cork and Killarney. Sure enough, a masked O'Boyle emerged from the undergrowth on horseback, yelling the common highwayman's refrain, "Stand and deliver." He was greeted, not with trembling victims or rich rewards, but with a hail of pistol balls. He fell from his escaping horse, shot through many times - dead. He had gone too far. He had become too immersed in, too enamored with, the "Rapparee" way of life; and I had led him into that way of life. Guilt washed over me when I heard the news. My friend from France, from Scotland, from our time in Ireland, was deceased. I was one of the few to attend his funeral, which cast some suspicion on me. I wrote to his family telling them that he died falling from a horse to spare them the bloody details of the truth. As for good friends, I now had none – only transactional acquaintances, including Ginny O'Neill.

It was clear to me that France and Great Britain were once more inching toward a war. Here and there, around the globe during the early 1750s, they sniped at one another. The outcome of the War of the Austrian Succession had satisfied neither party. It seemed that John was already caught up in a preliminary drama to a coming contest in America; and what would a new war in Europe mean for Ireland – historic friend to France but absent a strong 'Stuart' connection this time? Monsieur Boyer started to explore with me the possibility that a Jacobite rising, supported by France, might take place in Ireland. Boyer obviously had connections that went well beyond his trading (that is, smuggling) activities, all the way to Versailles. We discussed where French troops might "hypothetically" be landed in the event of a war, the number of muskets that would be needed by any rebel army, the key places that must be seized from the British, and just how many Jacobites might be enlisted in aid of any potential invasion and rebellion. Yet, fully engaged elsewhere, France did nothing. I grew restless. Boyer admonished me by saying, "Be patient. A plan is coming together at the highest levels in Paris, but we are not yet 'officially' at war with the English. When that contest is finally joined, Ireland will be flooded with French troops, muskets, munitions, and other supplies."

So, I waited. All of Catholic Ireland waited. Was the hour of our liberation almost at hand?

6. Gathering Storms

KILLARNEY, KERRY, 3RD OF AUGUST 1751.

"Are you a highway robber?" Ginny asked me one evening. I replied, "Why do you say that?" She said, "The money you present to me is not obtained from working as a mere cooper. If that trade paid so well, everyone would want to make barrels. And I know you claim to be an aristocrat, and you may have some inherited wealth, but I see you swapping items for payment in pounds with our French friend, Monsieur Boyer, who is in, let us say, the 'import and export' business. I know that your traveling companion, Mister O'Boyle, was shot to pieces trying to rob a coach on the road to Cork." I asked, "So that makes me a rogue, does it?" She replied, "You know what they say about 'birds of a feather' and how they flock." I said, "Would it make any difference to you if I was a highwayman?" She grinned and said, "No, but I would think if that were the case, you could afford to be more charitable with your close friends, like me." Always the greedy flower, Ginny was.

I laid low for a time after Sean O'Boyle was killed by the authorities. They raided his room in central Killarney, and while they found money secured from our raiding and robbing, nothing was found directly linking me to his (and my) nefarious activities. Still, informers told local law enforcers that I was witnessed attending O'Boyle's funeral and may be associated with that highwayman. British troops arrived at "McCarthy and Sons" and unceremoniously hauled me away to the local garrison for questioning. My room at the "Black Horse Inn" was torn apart as well. But after O'Boyle's death, I had taken precautions to hide away both my weapons and my stolen goods behind a false wall in the room that Boyer retained at the inn on an ongoing basis – and to which he had provided me with the whereabouts of the hiding spot for the room's additional key. The innkeeper, O'Connor, was briefly questioned by the authorities about me as well. He feigned ignorance: I was just a cooper, a patron, and a long-time resident at the inn as far as he was aware – nothing special, nothing more, not a trouble-maker. At the garrison, I was screamed at, punched, slapped, and accused of being a rebel and a traitor to the Crown. I put on a portrayal as being simply a humble barrel maker who came up from Cork to take advantage of an employment opportunity. I only knew O'Boyle as a traveling companion, nothing more. When no spoils from highway robberies were discovered in my room at the inn, the questioning trailed off, my interrogators lost interest, and I was finally released.

When I had free time on my hands, I decided to explore the road from Killarney to Tralee, a pleasant town in the north, I was told, and from there further north and east toward the city of Limerick. I was interested in seeing the location of our family's original estate and discovering in whose hands it might be now. The road to Tralee snaked through the mountains north of Killarney, close to the coast. While it was a remote area, I still met travelers occasionally. One was a Killarney area landowner, tax commissioner, and captain in the militia named Michael Farrell. He was traveling alone but was weighed down with books of account, strongboxes, and a pair of pistols in pockets slung on either side of his horse just in front of the saddle. I spoke with him for a bit and found him to be a thoroughly pompous and unpleasant fellow. But I made a note of how he behaved, reacted, and the fact that he made the six-league trip from Tralee to Killarney on a twice-monthly basis (mainly Thursdays). I carried no pistols of my own at the time, still playing the cautious rover after O'Boyle's death and my questioning by the British. I let him go on his way for now.

Tralee ("Tralgh Li" in Irish) was a fine town and the county seat, situated on the northern edge of the Dingle Peninsula, guarding the approaches from the north to mountains that ran south into Kerry. It was the site of a Norman castle, once the haven of the powerful Fitzgerald clan. The town was razed by Queen Elizabeth I's forces in the course of putting down an Irish rebellion in 1580.

Elizabeth I's efforts to pacify Ireland were nearly as brutal and bloody as Cromwell's. When the Norman-Irish rulers of the province of Munster revolted against her increasing intrusions upon their autonomy (and her attempts to impose Protestantism on their Catholic followers) during the "Desmond Rebellions," she struck back mercilessly against the Irish, whom she once called a "...rude and barbarous nation." Her generals crushed the Munster revolt in 1582, with upwards of 30,000 Irish killed in battle or dying of disease or starvation. Then came the so-called "Nine Years War," another revolt of Irish earls against Tudor domination that took place in various parts of the country. There were early Irish victories, with the English being pushed back to their old coastal 'Pale' and a few walled cities that they still held sprinkled around the country. But Elizabeth was not done: she assembled the largest army to ever leave England, which ultimately besieged the vital Irish-held port of Kinsale, near Cork. The English army routed the Irish defenders and their Spanish allies and took that port in what was considered a major victory at the time. Under renewed military pressure, many of the most militant earls in the north, including Ginny's relative in Ulster, Hugh O'Neill, 2nd Earl of Tyrone, fled to the continent in late 1607 in what was called the "Flight of the Earls." Their departure marked the beginning of Protestant 'plantation' control over Ulster, a slew of confiscations of Irish Catholic lands around the island, and, essentially, the beginning of the end of native Irish rule.

Shifting loyalties allowed the O'Finns to avoid a loss of their estate to Elizabeth I and even Cromwell, but they were not so lucky with William of Orange. Their lands were lost with the Treaty of Limerick in 1691 and the "Flight of the Wild Geese." I was determined to see who exactly was sleeping in our proverbial "bed" at the old estate. I stayed only one night in Tralee at the "Slieve Inn" and then headed northeast toward Limerick and the site of our ancestral home. Before leaving Tralee, I learned from some Limerick-bound travelers that a Scottish lord named Duncan now owned our old haunt, calling the place "Loch Lomond" after a location in Scotland. I found the estate and surveyed its environs, wondering if it should not be the site of my next "Rapparee" strike. Having no weapons on hand, however, I resolved to head back over the mountains to Killarney. Another time, perhaps.

When I returned to the "Black Horse," the innkeeper, O'Connor, informed me that a letter had been put into his hands from my master, old McCarthy. I opened the letter and it announced my termination from my trade as his cooper. The letter went on to say that while McCarthy had no quarrel with my work, the recent suspicions raised by the authorities that I might be a rebel or might know some rebels, or might be some sort of disreputable person, were enough for the coopers to let me go to protect the reputation of their trade. With apologies, my final pay was included with the post. It was a surprising blow but by no means catastrophic. My role as a cooper was more of a part I played than a serious trade. I still had funds with me or funds I could draw upon from my father's bequest. Of course, I could take to the highways again for "profit" should I be so inclined. My financial future was of no great concern to me. I paid up the inn's chamber rental for another month and started to plot my strategy for dealing with the land thief, Lord Duncan. Yet, before I could 'tweak the nose' of the Protestant aristocracy, I received a letter from Erin, which called for a more immediate response from me.

Erin indicated that she required my help. She had discovered, under the worst possible circumstances (having overheard their plotting), that her husband and her local avocat and trustee were in league. They had fired our steward, Rousseau, and had replaced him with an apathetic friend of O'Malley's. O'Malley and the avocat were now planning to subvert the 'trust' I had established before departing for Ireland in hopes of gaining full control over the Saint-André property. They also conspired to turf Erin out onto the road and replace her with some whore O'Malley had taken up with. I obviously did not have time to respond by return post but decided to go and see Monsieur Boyer, who I knew would be arriving back at the "Black Horse Inn" in two days' time. In the meanwhile, I set about making my own pistol charges. Black powder was poured into a paper cartridge that contained a lead ball, tied off in two places. When loading, the owner ripped open the tied-off cartridge paper, coated in lard, with one's teeth, primed the pistol's pan with some powder, then rammed the ball and remaining powder, paper and all, down the barrel with a ramrod. These hand-made cartridges were superior in every way to the old method of using a "powder horn" to administer all of the black powder needed to get the pistol ready to be fired. Preparing your own charges was a faster method of loading the weapon, and making such charges was one of the best skills that I learned during my time in the French army.

When Boyer finally arrived back at the inn following a trip to France, I informed him about my recent entanglements with the law, emphasizing that it did not seem to concern him very much, provided he was not implicated, which he was not. I then asked him if he could arrange for my transportation to and from France on one of the ships he used for smuggling contraband. He said, "I can get you out of Ireland and to the port of Brest through the port of Dingle—for a price." I replied, "I will pay you whatever is necessary to get there and back quickly." We discussed the arrangements and the remuneration, and I inquired about taking a pistol with me and the precautions that should be taken.

Boyer owned a vessel that was now bound for Dingle from France with smuggled goods aboard, and he agreed to accompany me to Dingle Harbor. He would provide the captain of the arriving ship with special instructions for my voyage to and from the continent. The vessel would then depart, landing me at Brest, France. From there, I would have to make my own way to Saint-André. Boyer identified a man in Brest who could help secure a horse for me.

I informed Ginny that I would be away for a while, without fully revealing my plans to her, including my destination. All she had to say was, "Well, bring me back something nice."

Boyer and I rode to Dingle Bay on a star-filled night, and upon arrival, I boarded my horse at a livery stable. I paid Boyer one-half of the price for the entire trip, and after discussing final details, I went aboard the ship headed for France. It was not a journey without risks. If a British vessel guarding the coasts were to stop this smuggling vessel, all aboard would likely be searched and arrested. If my story fell apart (and my pistol was found), I could face a hanging. This would be no enjoyable holiday visit. There was serious work to be done in France involving my family and our future.

7. France

BREST, FRANCE, 7TH OF JAMUARY 1752.

The crossing to Brest was rough, riding atop a raging winter sea. Waves crashed against the vessel and pounded the seawall at Brest, but we finally found some calm in the inner harbor at that place. Upon landing, I was briefly questioned by a totally disinterested French customs official and was dismissed. As instructed by Boyer, I went to see a man about a horse and, with my small collection of belongings and tools, headed out with my rented mount on the road to Saint-André. I stopped only once for a quick meal at a roadside "auberge" or inn, feeling as if I was being watched by the very suspicious-looking patrons, and then headed south once more.

Finally, I was "home" again at the estate I had not seen in years. I could tell that the grounds and buildings had not been well maintained and looked a bit shabby. Few laborers seemed to be about. Did anyone actually work on this estate? I knew from Erin's correspondence that she had left the chateau to escape her abusive husband and was staying at a friend's home on Rue Saint-Germain in Saint-André.

I rode up to the front doors of the chateau, secured my horse, and concealed my now-loaded pistol behind my cloak. I pounded on the door a number of times. After several minutes passed, a tired-looking, half-dressed, bleary-eyed man smelling of rum opened the door. "Yes?" he asked. I recognized the hint of an Irish brogue. "Is Monsieur O'Malley at home?" I asked. "That is me," he answered, "and who the blazes are you?" I recognized my sister's husband from the one time I had seen them together before I departed for Ireland. I said, "I, sir, am your worst nightmare." I produced my pistol and shot him in the face. I quickly climbed back aboard my horse and headed toward Saint-André for "Act Two" of my self-designed opera. I could hear the high-pitched scream of an unknown female coming from inside the chateau as I rode away.

My next stop was the office of the avocat, Monsieur Bernier, who I had originally hired and trusted with the management of my affairs while I was away in Ireland. He had betrayed both Erin and me for profit in league with Mister O'Malley. I entered his office, and the bespectacled avocat was sitting behind a desk, alone. "Can I help you?" he asked, hardly looking up. "Yes, please," I said, "there is something I wish to show to you." He stood up to come forward toward me, and I planted a loaded pistol against the middle of his forehead and cocked back the hammer. He recognized me at that time. "Monsieur Finn, what do you want?" he stammered. I said, "I want you to collect all of your paperwork on the 'trust' involving my estate outside of town and deliver it to my sister Erin at No. 12 Rue Saint-Germain. You are hereby discharged from our service. I am aware of what you and that miserable piece of shite, Monsieur O'Malley, have been up to. Your only hope to avoid prosecution by the authorities, or worse, is to do exactly as I say. If you hesitate in any way or continue to be involved in Erin's affairs, then you may very well end up like O'Malley." He choked up a bit and said, "And how has Monsieur O'Malley ended up?" I replied, "Go and ask him yourself at the chateau." I then left to conclude my business with Erin.

I found my sister at her friend's house on Rue Saint-Germain. She was overjoyed to see me, and we hugged. I asked to speak to her in private, and her friend graciously retreated from the room. I told Erin to expect a visit from the avocat, Bernier, and the nature of the files he would be carrying. I instructed her to take those files to a new and more trusted avocat and to reclaim and revive our estate as quickly as possible. I informed her that she might have to answer some difficult questions from the authorities about the fate of her philandering husband. She did not seem upset upon hearing of his passing. She assured me that she had plenty of witnesses regarding her whereabouts when he expired and would plead ignorance of any plot against him or even the fact of my visit. She also noted that we could absolutely trust her friend, Natalie, as well.

Erin and I chatted only briefly as I had to make my escape back to Brest for the return voyage to Ireland. Soldiers would soon be out on the roads looking for the murderer of Mister O'Malley. Erin indicated, among other things, that she had heard nothing concerning John or his current whereabouts. It was with extreme sadness that I left her this time, as I had a feeling that I would not see her for many more years to come. Gathering up some food for my return trip, I headed back to Brest in order to make Boyer's smuggling vessel. I returned my rented horse, made the ship in time, and we struck out on the return voyage to Dingle. But at the mouth of the channel, a Royal Navy sloop caught sight of us and gave chase. Boyer's fast smuggling ship was not to be outperformed, however, and she outran, then eluded, our pursuers. Boyer was in Dingle to meet me at the dock. "How was your visit to France?" he asked. "Productive," I said. Boyer slipped the harbor master some funds to 'smooth' the entrance of his suspect goods. I helped him load his contraband onto a well-guarded wagon, paid him the balance I owed him for my trip, and reclaimed my horse, "Mercury." We headed back on the road to Killarney.

Eventually, I received news from Erin by post. She indicated that, while she and her friend were vigorously questioned by the authorities, their pleas of ignorance were finally believed and accepted. Bernier delivered the paperwork I had demanded to Erin, begging her forgiveness as well. He said nothing to investigators about my visit to him, and the murder of O'Malley remained something of a local unsolved mystery in Saint-André (although there was some speculation that he was killed over a gambling debt). The relevant legal paperwork found its way to a trusted avocat. O'Malley's concubine and his steward were evicted from the estate, and Erin resumed control over the place. She was more in command now than ever before. Rousseau was rehired as steward, and everything seemed to have been set right. It only took a murder and an act of intimidation to accomplish those ends. Now it was time to set things right with Lord Duncan of Loch Lomond.

After a month or two cavorting with Ginny, drinking whiskey, and generally enjoying myself, I began to plan my revenge on Lord Duncan. In the spring, I made my way up the mountain roads to Tralee, then to Limerick, looking to gain an advantage over his lordship. From my surveillance, he seemed to have a routine each day: going by coach to Limerick, shopping or banking, and then going to an office he kept on the broad street. It seemed better to visit his lordship out on the highway with one (possibly armed) footman accompanying him and steering his coach than to try and confront him in a crowded town with armed soldiers all about. On the appointed day, I rode out to "Loch Lomond" and noted that both he and a woman I took to be Lady Duncan were heading for Limerick by coach. I went back to a spot I had picked out where a trail through the surrounding forest crossed the main road. The trail itself was secluded by trees. There were few travelers about on that section of the roadway at that time of day. Masked, with two pistols holstered near my saddle, I lay in wait for the Lord's coach to arrive. I heard the coach on the road before I saw it. I slowly moved out on "Mercury" to block the coach's progress, pointing one pistol at the footman driver with the other pistol close by in the holstered pocket and my rapier at my side. I yelled, "Stand and deliver."

The driver pulled up on the reins and then looked to a carbine tucked up close to him in a slot by his seat. "No, no, no," I said to the footman, "a pistol ball will put a terrible hole in a man." My statement got his attention, and he sat erect. As I started to move beside the coach on my horse, the irate Lord Duncan tried to open the coach door and jump out onto the road. With my foot, I violently shut the coach door. "Not until I tell you to get out," I commanded. I slowly moved back toward the front of the coach and ordered the footman to, first, hold the carbine by the barrel and then to pass it down to me. I told him that he was to remain in place and not to move. He complied admirably with my directions. I rode back to the side of the coach and ordered Lord and Lady Duncan out of the coach. Once Lord Duncan had helped his wife down to the road, he turned on me, declaring, "What do you think you are playing at, man? Do you know who I am? Do you know that you could hang for this?" I replied, "Obviously I am prepared to take my chances, or I would not be here." I told the footman to carefully throw down two small chests strapped to the roof of the coach, and for his lordship to turn out his pockets while the lady was to give over her purse and jewels. Lady Duncan was quite a lovely colleen, much younger than her husband. Lord Duncan screamed, "This is madness. My wife will not divest herself of her heirlooms." I angrily stood in my stirrups and said, "She will divest them, or maybe I should take her into the nearby forest and divest her of more than just her heirlooms. Now, here is a sack for your donations," which I threw to Lord Duncan. The pair started the process of divestment with a look of horror on their faces.

As I kept the pistol upon them, I heard the familiar sound of a donkey cart coming down the road. I let it approach and saw a shabbily dressed old man and a younger girl in rags riding in the cart, with bundles of hay as cargo. They hesitated for a moment as they drew close, but I waived them forward. Lord Duncan called out to them, "Save us from this rogue. Strike him down with something – a pitchfork or a hatchet." The cart driver just continued moving forward, and as he passed by, he said to me, "God bless you, sir." His lordship would receive no help from them. Soon, I had accumulated a massive haul: gold sovereigns, near-priceless jewels, all of their rings, and chests full of valuables. I took what I pleased, tucked up some gold pieces in my pocket, threw the carbine into the forest, and said to my victims, "As you have confiscated what the Irish owned, so too will your property be confiscated. I bid you a good day." I then tore off down the road on my horse. When I caught up with the impoverished pair in the donkey cart, I dug out some gold coins from my pocket and tossed them to the driver, declaring, "Éirinn go Brách" ("Ireland to the end of time" in Irish). I did not stop until I reached Killarney.

I secured some of my winnings from his lordship behind Boyer's false wall in his chamber but kept a full one-half of my rewards out and available to me. I invited Ginny up to my room for a jar of whiskey. She finally complied around midnight, and we sat talking and drinking. Finally, I produced the sack I had refilled in the wake of the Limerick robbery and poured out those remaining contents onto the small table around which we sat. "Is this enough to buy some 'exclusivity' for our relationship?" I asked. Ginny fingered through the spoils in awe and declared, "Yes, yes, I think I can be yours alone now. You are too good to me. You really do care for me." I said, "It is a bargain then. Let us seal it with a kiss." We kissed madly, then copulated like rabbits. It was splendid. Ginny seemed genuinely happy.

My attack on Lord Duncan caused a flurry of concern among the authorities: a peer of the realm had been waylaid and robbed, and something must be done about it. A 500-pound reward was offered for information leading to the arrest of the masked rogue who dared upset a lord and his lady. However, searches and inquiries seemed to be concentrated around the Limerick area and to the west and northwest of that place. The masked rogue who carried out the bold raid was not discovered, and I went on about my ordinary affairs.

I felt comfortable enough in my relationship with Ginny to tell her I was, indeed, a highwayman (as if she did not already know). She delighted in the spoils I could bring her from my "Rapparee" exploits, and she encouraged me to take to the roads and scoop up more profits whenever she fell a little short of the finer things in life. I warned her not to flaunt any ill-gotten wealth, or she would end up like O'Boyle. She promised to be prudent. As time went by, however, I began to grow leery of Ginny's interactions with other wealthy gentlemen. I even suspected liaisons between Ginny and Boyer. I once saw her emerging from his room, although he was not in residence at the time but was in France. Were these legitimate concerns or simply jealous imaginings? Ginny swore fidelity to me, and I never delved too deeply into what might be behind her flirtatious ways.

As war with France seemed to be becoming more likely, Great Britain shifted a number of new regiments into Ireland to guard against the old French or Spanish trick of throwing an expeditionary military force into Ireland to threaten England with invasion and spark a rebellion among the Catholic population. All these new (and old) British formations had to be garrisoned, clothed, fed, and paid (although British soldiers were forced to use much of their pay to reimburse the crown for many necessaries they were provided, including bread, medical care, and beer). I began to think that if I could rob a British Army pay wagon, I would not only be awash in money but would strike one more blow for Irish freedom. Pay for the southern British garrisons came from Dublin through the port of Cork and was then disbursed accordingly. While I secured a new trade at a local Killarney brewer, "Killarney Beer and Wines," to maintain the façade that I had lawful employment, I found time to travel down to Cork to determine how, when, and where the army pay was moved. After careful scrutiny, it seemed that pay wagons fanned out from the Cork garrison to Waterford, Limerick, Killarney, and every garrison south of the Shannon River. A barman in Cork informed me that civilian paymasters, under the supervision of the colonels of the various regiments, actually dispensed the pay when it reached the respective garrisons. Normally, a pay wagon was manned by at least four guards, including the teamster, and a squad of dragoons followed behind. If I were to attack such a formidable crew, killings would be required as part of the action, and some means of separating the wagon from the dragoon escort must be found (as I was not prepared to take on a whole complement of cavalry by myself).

And as war in Europe drew ever closer, Monsieur Boyer began spending more time in Killarney, engaged in God-knows-what kind of skulduggery. We still spoke to one another concerning French plans for the war, and I undertook to seek out what Jacobites I could find in contemplation of a future uprising. One such patriot was a Protestant doctor in Killarney, Doctor Best, who was inspired to fight for the liberty of all Irishmen, Catholic and Protestant alike, should it come to that. But one had to be extremely careful when recruiting potential Jacobite rebels, as there were many informers tucked up among the population. One wrong word could potentially send you to the gallows. I also imposed upon Boyer to provide me with a few kegs of black powder, as my plan for the army pay robbery was starting to come together. He knew by now not to even ask what I might be up to with the powder. He secured the required kegs.

By 1754, fighting between France and Great Britain had already broken out in several places in the backcountry of America, including Nova Scotia, where John was stationed. Once that happened, Boyer informed me that he would actually spend less time in Ireland, as the British hunt for French spies was already on, and the sea lanes were being swarmed by Royal Navy vessels. However, he kept his room at the "Black Horse Inn" for my benefit (as a hiding place for stolen property, guns, and powder) and for his benefit (occasional but risky visits and storing essential supplies in case a French plan for an invasion of Ireland came together). O'Connor was greedy enough to take rent from a guest who was rarely there, but he also ensured that no one ever bothered with Boyer's particular chamber (although I knew where the spare key to the room was hidden - and apparently, so did Ginny).

My plan for collecting the army pay revolved around destroying a wooden bridge over a deep gully on the Cork Road, thereby separating the dragoons from the army pay wagon. Once that happened, the real violence would take place: I would have to speed down the road, kill four soldiers with pistol and rapier, and collect the army pay, making my escape cross-country. Timing would be everything because it would not take long for the dragoons to find a way around my roadblock. Or if I got into an extended fight with the wagon's guardians, my whole plan might fall apart. During the afternoon before my maraud, I set out for the targeted bridge near Cork with two kegs of gunpowder and fuses. I climbed down below the bridge at dusk and set up my 'bombs' in strategic places on its timber supports, just as I had learned that skill in the army. Twice I had to snuff out my small lantern and hide, avoiding carriages rolling over the bridge. By daybreak, my trap was set, my horse was hidden but well-positioned on the Killarney side of the bridge, and the explosives were arranged to go off after the nearby fuses were lit. Now, I had to wait for the pay wagon – which was always regular and on-time - to appear.

Waiting to commit murder would be murder itself.

8. Calamity

The pay wagon came rolling up to and over the bridge on the Cork Road, heading in the direction of Killarney. The dragoon escort was not far behind, but by then, the fuses were lit. One - then a second - blast shook the air. The immediate area was clouded in black powder smoke, but it appeared from what I could see that the bridge was left in somewhat of a shambles. The dragoons now looked as if they were cut off from the pay wagon. I hiked up my mask, vaulted onto my horse, and rode off toward the now-speeding wagon. I gave no warning as I thundered toward the wagon, with the reins of the bridle between my teeth and both pistols out and ready. I shot one guard, then another, off the rear of the wagon, trampling one soldier in the process. I quickly holstered my pistols and drew my rapier, stabbing first, the teamster, then grabbing the teamster's seat and leaping aboard the careening wagon. I ran through the other startled guard. So far, so good, but no sooner had I grabbed the reins and brought the wagon to a halt, out of the smoke and dust, up the road came a formation of charging dragoons! How did they avoid my obstacle so quickly?

I would now have no time to loot the wagon. I would barely have enough time to make my escape. I sheathed my rapier, jumped on "Mercury" and spurred him forward. Then the lead started flying, filling the air. I

"

caught a ball in my side as "Mercury" pulled away from our pursuers. I veered off into a meadow, urged "Mercury" to leap a stream, then over a fence, and I moved off into some brush. Finally, I found a forest trail I could follow. Once I was satisfied that the dragoons were no longer a concern, I quickly headed off to Killarney in order to secure medical attention.

Not every physician could be trusted to treat a wound like I had received; I went straight to the Jacobite physician, Doctor Best, who took me in and assured me that my wound was only in the 'fleshy' parts, was not that serious, and would heal quickly. He removed the ball, burned and bandaged the wound, and sent me on my way. I could rely on him to say nothing to the authorities. When I returned to the "Black Horse Inn," Ginny fawned over and cared for me. I rested up and drank whiskey while the British army scoured the countryside looking for the "murdering rebel scum" who had dared attack the Crown's pay wagon and killed four soldiers. As bounties had not encouraged local people to come forward in the past with information on "Rapparees," terror would now have to be employed to wring information out of them. Suspected Jacobites were rounded up in Cork, Killarney, as far north as Tipperary and as far south as Kinsale. Beatings, whippings, and threats involving family members were used to 'convince' these prisoners of the British to cooperate. When nothing could be gleaned from those captives, the British convinced themselves that the highwayman responsible for the Cork Road ambush must have escaped to France. Doctor Best and I avoided interrogation entirely, although once before, in the wake of Sean O'Boyle's killing, I had been similarly questioned by the army.

Once the frenzy over the attempted army pay robbery died away, I took an opportunity to head out toward Cork to see if I could discover what went wrong with my ambush of the pay wagon. The wooden bridge I had blasted was being rebuilt when I arrived, but a local farmer who had witnessed the aftermath of my explosions explained to me that while much of the bridge collapsed, enough of it remained for some dragoons to pick their way across the dangerous skeleton of the bridge with their mounts and charge up the road. He whispered, "Damn those 'lobsters' [what the Irish sometimes called the British soldiers, given their red frocks with tails], they prevented the highwayman from securing the army gold. But that Irish hero gave the British a bloody nose." I was not really in the business of simply administering "bloody noses" to the British; however, I had hoped to profit from my dangerous attempted robbery. Next time, I hoped.

My effort at robbing the pay wagon happened during a period of increasing tensions in Ireland. As the possibility of a French invasion loomed with France and Great Britain lurching toward a full-blown war, rural violence, especially in the south of Ireland, was sparked intermittently by restrictive government land and tax policies. A secret Irish society called the "Whiteboys" (named after the white smocks they wore), featuring late-night meetings and swearing sacred blood oaths, came together to intimidate Protestant landowners, keep Catholics on the land, destroy unwanted fences and outbuildings, steal muskets for self-defense, and occasionally free wrongfully detained citizens. They portrayed themselves as 'ghost-like' avengers who could strike the authorities quietly, at will, then disappear into the dark of night. While their efforts were only a nuisance to the authorities at first, the Whiteboys became bolder, more militant, and more effective as time went by. Combined with the efforts of the "Rapparees," the Protestant establishment began to worry about losing control over rural Ireland at a most dangerous time.

War! In 1756, the smoldering conflict between France and Great Britain in America helped spark a far-flung European conflict. While I was pleased to see this new contest explode between Catholic and Protestant alliances, it concerned me that John was apparently still battling French and Indian forces overseas. Monsieur Boyer could now only rarely brave a British blockade of the French coast and always made his way toward remote and dangerous landings on the Dingle Peninsula (for coming directly into Dingle Harbor was now far too dangerous). As for me, I took to the highways less frequently given an increase in British patrols, and Ginny complained more frequently about the scarcity of money and gifts coming her way. Still, our relationship remained relatively strong and stable, I thought. Boyer, meanwhile, assured me that the French were still coming to free Ireland, but they must first collect sufficient resources, sweep the British Navy from the seas, and save their colonies in America, especially their valuable Caribbean sugar islands.

But the French did not come.

France was actually planning a major invasion of Great Britain proper, not Ireland, with up to 100,000 troops. They enlisted the help of the mostly-discredited Prince Charles Edward Stuart – "Bonnie Prince Charlie" – to once again help raise a new Jacobite army using his now-frayed contacts in the British Isles. He was reportedly summoned to Paris to meet the French Foreign Minister and discuss the plan, but he failed to impress as he railed about past French betrayals and a current lack of obvious support for any Jacobite uprising. The French then entirely dispensed with Prince Charles's help and pushed ahead with their own invasion strategies. Those plans crashed against the rocks of the British naval victory at Quiberon Bay in 1759, which rendered a French invasion of Great Britain all but impossible.

The only time that French actions caused a stir in Ireland was when a French privateer, Francois Thurot, who had served in the Irish Brigade (and may have been half-Irish), started seizing British ships along the Irish coast and briefly made a landing in Donegal. In February 1760, after further misadventures, he even landed and seized the old 12th-century Norman castle stronghold of Carrickfergus, near Belfast, but was forced to flee as a flotilla of British warships approached. Thurot's shenanigans proved to be France's only invasion of Ireland during the so-called "Seven Years War." In America, the war was also drawing to a close with major British victories in New France. But just when I hoped that John would survive the war and return to Ireland, Great Britain and Spain, its old adversary, went to war in early 1762, and John's regiment was sent to fight in the ultimately successful but disease-plagued siege of Havana, Cuba. By 1763, the 40th Regiment of Foot was back in Nova Scotia, not Ireland. I did not know whether John was dead or alive.

The war was but one more calamity for the Jacobite cause. The ties that once bound Prince Charles to his supporters in Great Britain and Ireland were all but severed. While still referring to the movement to end the British occupation of Ireland as "Jacobite," it was not really of that character anymore: it had evolved into more of a 'national independence' movement, pushing away from its Catholic-monarchical roots. It soon started to take inspiration from a philosophically similar movement taking shape in the Thirteen American colonies: mildly anti-monarchist, in favor of self-government, against burdensome taxation, and trumpeting the liberty of all men. Ironically, this philosophy arose out of France and Spain's defeat in the Seven Years War. Those old allies of convenience of the Irish were now found to be unable to assist Jacobites in Ireland in any substantial way during the war and ultimately were humbled and defeated by the growing power of Great Britain, master of the seas.

Ireland was, more and more, forced to look inward to its own devices in pursuit of its liberty.

9. Betrayal

KILLARNEY, KERRY, 4TH OF APRIL 1763.

Ginny O'Neill was testy. I had only taken to the highways occasionally during the Seven Years War to feather our collective nest. Now, with the Peace of Paris (February 1763) and an overwhelming British victory against France and Spain, which gave the British nation new confidence at home and abroad, the tensions that arose over a possible French invasion of Ireland dissipated. The British military presence was reduced somewhat in Ireland, which opened up new possibilities for raiding and robbing the Protestant establishment. I began to consider new targets for my thieving, and my mind kept going back to the landlord and tax commissioner, Captain Farrell, whom I had encountered on the mountain road to Tralee back in 1751. If he was still making his periodic trips over the Slieve Mish Mountains with his strongboxes full of coins, his status as a collector of the Crown's dues and the wealth that he carried both made him an inviting object for my attentions. I made trips up to Tralee several times to see if I could discover this self-important Crown official but did not find him.

It was not unusual for men like Farrell to be collectors of the King's taxes. Appointed by the Crown to collect revenues in their home district, they were both feared and hated for enforcing unpopular measures such as the collection of tithes (through his appointment by the Church of

Ireland), the stamp tax, the poll tax, taxes on goods and services. They obtained their tax collection commissions through their association with the Protestant establishment and then profited greatly from them. I learned a while back that Farrell was not only a tax commissioner but a militia captain and landlord as well. He was once in the regular army and fought at both Falkirk and Culloden with the 8th Regiment of Foot. Rewarded by the Crown with a militia appointment and land in Ireland, Farrell, like the other resident and many absentee Protestant landlords in Ireland, pulled a full one-quarter of the value of the whole Irish economy (almost a million pounds a year) out of the Irish common folk in the form of rents on their overvalued tenancies. Some agricultural land was even turned into more profitable grazing lands, and many longtime farmers were evicted and displaced altogether. The forests were cut down, and iron pulled from the ground in England's haste to strip Ireland of her wealth. Several weather-related famines swept across Ireland during the mid-1700s, devastating the farming population further. Add to this, the Irish were forced to support the infrastructure and establishment of the Protestant Church of Ireland to which almost none of them belonged. Unless one was a serf in Russia, there were few people more downtrodden than the Irish farmer.

Such abuses gave rise to a sudden spasm of "Whiteboy"-orchestrated violence beginning in the spring of 1761, just before the end of the Seven Years' War. This new unrest spread over an area covering Waterford, Cork, Limerick, and Tipperary (and a similar protest movement opposed to ever-increasing local fees and tithes emerged around the same time in County Armagh led by the agrarian "Oakboys" society). In an effort to stamp out these rural rebellions, in April 1761, a military force was constituted under the leadership of the Marquess of Drogheda and was first sent to Munster Province in order to crush the Whiteboys' insurrection. Hundreds of suspects were rounded up (and I barely escaped that widening net myself), some were killed in skirmishes with the army, and a local priest was hanged in Clonmel, allegedly for supporting aspects of the rising. A 300-pound reward was made available for the capture of the leader of the Whiteboys and 50 pounds for each of his sub-lieutenants. The wide-ranging crackdown caused local farmers to abandon their fields and run for hiding spots in the mountains, leaving their farms in the hands of spouses and the elderly who could not cope with running them. Production dropped dramatically, local famines set in again, and politicians called for an end to the pacification effort as being unproductive and also because of its sheer ruthlessness.

The establishment's focus on the Whiteboys was over by 1763, as was the "French scare" over the possible invasion of Ireland. Due to the war and the Whiteboys insurgency, a heightened military presence had largely kept me off the highways and byways of southern Ireland. Now it was time to get back in the saddle. I retrieved my pistols and rapier from Monsieur Boyer's secret hiding spot, employed a 'domino mask' across the eyes (as a replacement for the half-face mask I used to wear) and hit the Cork road once more at dusk. I ambushed a coach carrying passengers mid-way to Killarney, but one of those travelers had a small concealed pistol and nervously took a shot at me after the stop. "Mercury" reared up, but both I and my horse avoided injury. By rights, I should have shot my assailant in revenge, but he proved to be such a pathetic character that I simply struck him with my pistol, robbed him and the other passengers of a wholly inadequate amount, and struck out for home. It was an unsatisfactory beginning. Was I losing my "touch" as a highwayman?

Ginny was sullen when I returned to the inn. I could tell that she was unhappy with the amount of the spoils gained on this occasion of thieving. We drank a jar of whiskey together, and she mentioned that Boyer was back from France and up in his chamber. I finished my drink and went to see the Frenchman. Boyer, too, was sullen: the war was lost, France's grand invasion schemes had come to naught, and he was probably more at risk of arrest for his smuggling activities than ever before. "I may as well pack it in and dispense with this cat-and-mouse game I have been playing with the British," Boyer said. "Sooner or later, I will end up dinner for the cat," he went on to say.

"Nonsense," I said, "the end of the war will only open up new opportunities for both you and me. Very soon the English will grow tired of hunting for French spies, will reduce the size of their military, and will go back to turning a blind eye to smuggling. There is money to be made. Why allow someone else to make it?" He pondered my response then chimed in, "Maybe you are right. I am just depressed over the loss of the war and the scuttling of our plans for a rebellion in Ireland. I have to get back to business and forget about politics." I cheerfully said, "I concur. Now let us get drunk!" And we did.

Unsatisfied with my last attempt at reviving my career as a highwayman, I undertook a few 'house breaks' that hardly netted me anything at all and simply got a Church of Ireland clergyman knocked on the head when he discovered me in his rectory. I then returned to coach robbing and secured a modest amount from a lone female traveler being driven to Killarney by her nervous footman. She was quite beautiful, and I considered for a moment stealing a kiss from her besides her purse, but I was not that sort of rogue and played the gentleman throughout the course of the robbery. But my thoughts kept returning to Captain Farrell. I recalled his travel schedule, and if I adhered to it (and he was still off robbing the poor of Ireland), then maybe someday we would cross paths. I also considered revisiting my unsuccessful army pay wagon robbery scheme, but finding Farrell seemed the easier (and less risky) of the two options, and I started to explore the road to Tralee through those famous Kerry mountains once more.

My persistence finally paid off. Early one Thursday morning as I came up over a steep rise on the trail north to Tralee, I briefly caught sight of a horse and a seated gentleman whom I recognized immediately. It was Captain Farrell. I retreated a bit, put on my mask, checked my pistols for sufficiency (one of which I holstered and one I carried), then slowly moved up the rise. The area was remote, and I had not met another traveler in some time. Captain Farrell sat on a rock with a camp table beside him and strongboxes all around him. Best of all, money was piled high on the small table upon which he was counting and then entering the numbers into his ledgers with a quill and ink. His horse was tied to a tree at a distance, and his pistols were visible, tucked up in front of his saddle in twin holsters. He was vulnerable. I had the advantage over him.

Dressed up in riding boots, a dark-colored vest, cloak, and a cocked hat, the portly Farrell raised an eyebrow, then turned to look at me slowly approaching over the rise. He cast a quick glance at his pistols and realized that he would never make it to them before I shot him. I rode closer, steering my horse with my knees, pointing my pistol at him, then barking, "Stand and deliver" and drawing my rapier from its scabbard. Farrell growled, "Do you realize who you are trifling with? I am Captain Michael Farrell, a collector of the King's taxes, and most of these funds are bound for His Majesty's treasury. If you abscond with any of these monies, you will be hunted down like a dog by all of the forces available to the Crown." I replied, "Those funds were wrenched from the people of Ireland at the point of a gun. You like to tell the poor farmers who you forced to hand over their last farthings that the exercise of collecting taxes is for their own benefit; but those funds are collected so that your King can build more grand buildings and monuments to himself, pay more soldiers to oppress Ireland, and help English landlords grow fat off the bounty provided by Irish land. You, like the traitors who sit in the English Parliament, and their lackeys in the Irish Parliament, are simply bold deceivers."

I sheathed my rapier as I descended from "Mercury," all the while keeping my pistol on Farrell. Once I was on the ground, I drew out my rapier again. I demanded of him to, "Move away from the table, but to your left, well away from your horse." He complied yet watched me closely in a manner that suggested to me he would use any opportunity to attack me, escape, or both. I went over to the tax receipts, and the obvious amounts were huge. I stuffed my pockets full of coins and used a sack to collect the remainder as I did not want jangling strongboxes to be hanging from my horse as I rode away. I then ordered the Captain to, "Open the remaining boxes and money bags so that I can have a look inside." Farrell scowled and said, "I would rather die, you black-hearted bastard." I smiled and said, "That can easily be arranged. I killed your kind at Culloden and stacked up their bodies like firewood. Do you really think I would show you any mercy if you pushed me?" Mumbling curses under his breath, Farrell opened the remainder of the boxes and bags. I was stunned. They were each bulging with every manner of coin used in the British realms – pounds, pence, gold sovereigns, Spanish and French coins – a treasure trove. I backed Captain Farrell away from the money and collected up those proceeds. I said, "Carrying this amount of money, you should have had an armed escort." He replied, "The King is my armed escort, and he will be coming for you."

Once I had Farrell's money secured aboard "Mercury," I collected up his pistols and slapped the arse of his horse to make it bolt down the road in the direction of Tralee. I sheathed my rapier once again and bid the captain goodbye. He cried out, "You are going to leave me here in this wild country, forced to walk to Tralee? You may as well have killed me rather than abandon me helpless and in disgrace." I replied, "That can still happen, for I have no intention of accompanying you to any destination you might select; but eventually your horse will stop running, and you may retrieve it and make your way back to some village or town. The choice is yours. I can run you through right now, wipe my blade of your blood, and leave you in the dust if that is what you would prefer." He said nothing. I said, "I thought not. Goodbye, Captain Farrell, and God bless the Catholic heirs of good King James the Second." I threw the last reference into the conversation just to taunt him and emphasize that it was a Jacobite who had robbed him. I then rode off in the direction of Killarney.

As I arrived back at the "Black Horse Inn" in the early afternoon, I stabled my horse, entered through a rear area, then up some back stairs and straight into Boyer's room in order to hide away my stash of coins. Boyer was away on a smuggling trip to France but was due back the next afternoon. My take from the highway robbery and my weapons went behind Boyer's false wall, and I then went downstairs to see if Ginny was about. She was there, and I asked her to come to my room and bring a jar of whiskey with her when she was able. She hurriedly replied that she would see me in about an hour's time as she skirted with drinks between waiting patrons. I went back to Boyer's room, took out a large amount of money from my hiding place, then laid on my bed and waited for my partner. I was quite tired after the day's activities; robbery is hard work on occasion. Ginny appeared in an hour, as promised.

"Hello, my red-haired beauty," I chirped. "You are certainly in a good mood," Ginny replied. I said, "I have reason to be in a good mood, and so do you." She said, "Oh? And why is that?" I then smiled and said,

"Behold our fortune," as I poured out the contents of the sack I had partially reloaded in Boyer's room. Ginny gasped, then sighed, "This is all for me?" I replied, "Absolutely!" She then asked, "Is there more?" The question puzzled me a bit, but I said, "Much more, that we can both live on for a time." She then asked, "Why not buy our own house? There are some lovely cottages around Killarney." Ginny had taken to sharing a small cottage with another barmaid, and maybe that was more to her liking than being at the inn all the time. "We will see," I said. She then surprised me even more by saying, "How is it you get to make all of our important decisions? I only get to decide when we will take a tumble in the blankets." I shot back, "Because I am the one staring down the barrels of pistols to secure this kind of money. Do you know I took the chance of robbing a local tax commissioner, Captain Farrell, this last time around? He could have shot me, and the British army may yet kill me as they pursue the now-famous 'Rapparee' of the Tralee Road who was brave enough to deprive the English King of his blood money."

Ginny let the topic go but seemed a bit upset by our exchange. We drank some whiskey and engaged in some rapid copulation. After we were done, as we lay in bed, I felt the urge to ask her, "Am I still the only man you have been with since we made our bargain?" She replied, "Of course." I then asked, "You would never deceive or betray me, would you?" She declared, "Never." It sounded trustworthy enough, but who really knows what is in the heart of another? Ginny had a way of making me feel uneasy. "I have to go," Ginny suddenly said. She rose up from the bed, dressed quickly, and left. I lay in the bed wondering what my next robbery should entail: maybe something more spectacular than the robbery of the tax commissioner. I had a vision of raiding the Customs House in Cork. The proceeds would be awesome, and a successful strike would shock the 'Protestant Ascendancy' to their very core. The raid would take extraordinary planning and must not end up in an O'Boyle-style failure. The robbery itself must be timed to the minute, and my escape, even more so: it must not suddenly collapse like the pay wagon attack. As I trailed off to sleep, I dreamed of the riches a successful Customs House robbery could bring: gold and jewels, and maybe Ginny could even buy that cottage after all! I planned to make my way to Cork the very next morning in order to look over the Customs House and the strength of its protections.

Early the next morning, just before I rose to travel to Cork, I heard voices outside of my chamber's open window. A commotion of some sort was taking place in the courtyard of the inn; then a man suddenly yelled from the gathering crowd below, "Look what is coming. It is the whole damned British army!" I quickly looked out my window. It was not the army coming, but a formation of armed footmen led by none other than Captain Farrell himself! My first thought: I have been betrayed. I threw on a shirt and breeches and ran for Boyer's room to secure my pistols and rapier and avoid capture through a fight, if necessary. I secured Boyer's spare key, opened the door, went to the false wall hiding place, and found my rapier gone. Next, I opened up my cartridge box and found that every single cartridge was devoid of black powder and had been soaked in water, rendering them useless. I was at Farrell's mercy. I heard his footmen on the main stairs, so I ran for the back stairs. They, too, were crowded with footmen. As I turned to consider an alternate escape route, one large footman was already upon me. I struck him hard in the jaw, and it stunned him, but several more men were quick to assist him and grab me. I was pushed to the floor and bound. I was their prisoner.

Tied up with rope, I was marched into the courtyard of the inn in order to face Captain Farrell. He stood there, hands on his hips, chuckling to himself, and then said, "I knew I would find you. You are simply a stupid, thieving Jacobite piece of dog excrement." The captain went on to say, "It only took me a few hours after I was rescued by friendly horsemen on the Tralee Road to find your sorry backside. Now you can bow down before me in the dust and beg for my forgiveness." I replied, "Pox on you. Ask my bollocks." Farrell frowned and said, "Take him to the gaol." I was off for imprisonment. What had gone wrong? The truth would be hard to take.

10. Escape

KILLARNEY, KERRY, 30TH OF APRIL 1763.

As I sat in the local gaol, pondering my fate, the jailer came to my box of a cell and informed me that I had a visitor. The jailer searched the man, then opened the cell door to let him enter, careful all the while to keep a rigid wooden club handy just in case an escape attempt was made. My visitor was Brendan O'Connor, the owner of the inn. He was hanging his head in obvious shame. I had no visitors in the days prior to his arrival and since my arrest.

O'Connor began by saying, "First, I may as well tell you that you have lost your work as a tradesman at 'Killarney Beer and Wines.' They informed me this morning that you were dismissed when their courier came by to see me at the inn. My second bit of news is a little more tragic," and he hesitated. I was not concerned about the loss of a second employment I did not really rely upon to sustain me. I was anxious, however, to hear his 'second bit of news.' He went on to say, "The other afternoon, after Ginny left your chamber, she decided to go to the estate of the district tax commissioner, Captain Farrell, for she had been told by you that you were the rogue who had robbed Farrell on the Tralee Road. After arriving at his manor, she was introduced to the captain, recently returned from the road to Tralee, and upon claiming she had important information, was asked by Farrell to state her business. After making inquiries, she discovered that he was prepared to offer a £1000 reward for any information leading to the arrest of the bandit who had robbed him of his tax receipts. Ginny not only knew that you were the bandit he was looking for but also knew that, apart from the spoils you had already shared with her, a large and valuable amount of stolen goods, money, and weapons still sat behind the false wall in Monsieur Boyer's room - and she wanted it all, if she could get it.

Ginny offered to reveal the identity and location of the highwayman involved in the captain's robbery in return for not merely the reward he was prepared to offer but possession of all of the illegal money and merchandise on hand, other than the remaining hidden tax receipts. Farrell balked at first, threatened Ginny with arrest and that she would lose everything if she did not immediately reveal who had attacked him. But – as you well know – Ginny can be very stubborn. She then offered to "sweeten the pot" by also promising to reveal the identity of a French spy and smuggler operating in Killarney. Captain Farrell quickly summoned the local army garrison commander, and, by nightfall, the two had agreed in writing to Ginny's terms before a local magistrate. She then made her revelations, and the officials resolved on a strike against you and, later, Mister Boyer. Meanwhile, as you slept, Ginny returned to the 'Black Horse,' stole away your rapier, and destroyed your cartridges. She then went back to warn Farrell to take care as you were still quite accomplished with both pistols and rapiers, and if you obtained either, a slaughter may result. Accordingly, you were arrested by a large armed party of Farrell's men, and Boyer was ambushed by the army as well upon his return to the inn from a smuggling venture. His ships and merchandise have all been seized, and it does not look good for him. Ginny has not been back to work. I do not know where she is now or if I will avoid the widening circle of arrests. She assured me before she fled the inn that I was safe."

I was shocked to my very soul, but the story rang true. All the details of his narrative fit with what I knew of events as they unfolded - the stolen rapier, the destroyed cartridges, the sudden appearance of Farrell and his men right at my doorstep. If O'Connor was to be believed (and there was no obvious reason to doubt him), I had been betrayed by the one person with whom I had slowly built an emotional bond. What greed, what hypocrisy! A filthy, backstabbing traitor. I asked O'Connor if Ginny had indicated to him why she had informed on me. He replied, "She only said that you treated her more like a whore than a partner." My anger began to build. If I could get free, it would not be good for Ginny O'Neill. I told O'Connor not to trust Ginny's assurances and to beware. But I suspected that while he was now betraying Ginny, she had probably shared some of her 'good fortune' with him before leaving the inn.

I was once more beaten, berated, and vigorously questioned at the local army garrison about the raids initiated by various "Rapparees" in southern Ireland. Some I had been involved with, some not. I again feigned a degree of ignorance and innocence: I admitted to Farrell's robbery but pretended that I had come across him several years ago on the Tralee Road and planned the robbery over the course of those years. I had no involvement in other highway robberies and was no "Rapparee" or political bandit. Was I a Jacobite? Of course not. Was my profession that of a thief? No, I had worked at several honest, legitimate trades. The raid on Captain Farrell was just a single occurrence and took place because it was simply too tempting, and I was in need of funds.

My interrogators scoffed at my defense, claiming that Ginny had told them a very different story: that I was indeed a highway raider involved in many notable robberies. I told them that, of course, Ginny would spin such a tale to catch the interest of the authorities and justify her betrayal of a small-time bandit. The only way to secure a large reward was for Ginny to portray me as a "big fish" in the highwaymen's "pond." If there was a treasure trove of stolen goods in Boyer's chamber, I said, the treasure belonged to Boyer alone. In one sense, this was true, for Boyer did not keep stolen goods he received from me for very long but quickly converted goods into coins and then shipped the goods off to France. I clearly was not believed by those questioning me, but I was not sure that the authorities could prove otherwise.

I sat in the gaol until it was time for me to appear before a justice of the peace in Killarney. Eventually, the justice of the peace would determine at a preliminary inquiry if there was sufficient evidence to send my case to a grand jury for endorsement. I was to be charged with high treason, insurrection, and grand theft by robbery. If the charges were endorsed by the grand jury (that is, sufficient in terms of form and evidence), I would be tried before a justice, sitting with a petty jury, at the Court of Assizes in Tralee, the county seat. The hurdles of the preliminary inquiry and grand jury were both cleared, and I was set to appear before the Assizes.

The "common law" by which I would be tried was the Normans' "gift" to Ireland. Over time, it slowly eroded the application of Irish "Brehon" law, which was developed in ancient Gaelic times. Brehon law was Irish customary law administered first by Druids and later by 'brother' (or 'brithern') arbitrators. By the 7th century, this oral law, maintained by the brithern, had been reduced to writing. Brehon law was focused on restitution, not retribution, as opposed to the 'hammer' applied by the common law. It was a much more liberal system than the common law that treated genders equally under the law and provided for couples to divorce. There was no "death penalty" under Brehon law, and the goal was to make both victims and offenders 'whole' once again, bringing the parties to a realization of what each had suffered or done.

At first confined to the Norman (later English) "Pale" territory centered on Dublin, the common law expanded with the English armies. It became entrenched with England's religious split from Rome under the

Tudors and, later, Cromwell's destruction of the monasteries. Brehon law was fully usurped, and the "Penal Laws" made the application of the common law in Ireland very harsh. But Irish country folk still utilized Brehon law to settle local, civil disputes. Its application faded but did not entirely disappear.

While I awaited my trial before the Assizes, I was held at "Old Bridge Gaol" in Tralee. I was brought to the court for my pleas, pled "not guilty" to all charges, and a trial date was set for the summer of 1764. Ginny and Farrell would be the main witnesses against me, with the charges of treason and insurrection mainly being based on statements attributed to me by Farrell. When the time came to testify at trial, Ginny appeared but was shaking, nervous, and seemed uncertain. Suddenly, she only knew about the robbery of Captain Farrell, and only from what I had confessed to her, nothing more. She had no independent evidence of this, or any other robbery, and described my act of thievery as "impulsive." She testified that I was but a one-time minor outlaw with no political connections, from what she understood. She also claimed that she never profited from my robbery. My counsel, Mister Hobbs, turned her into a very friendly witness with his questioning. Captain Farrell, on the other hand, was spitting fire, swearing that I was a "Rapparee" in league with other Jacobites, that my robbery of a crown official was in aid of a planned insurrection, and that I had threatened and abused him in the course of the robbery. However, as I was wearing a mask over my eyes, his identification evidence was poor, and his memory of some events and statements I was said to have made was equally poor. I did not testify in my own defense on the advice of my counsel.

I did not know at the time that the presiding justice, Lamont, was a long-time rival of Captain Farrell and detested the man. He provided a sympathetic charge to the jury, and the jury found me guilty of grand theft by robbery but neither the treason nor insurrection crimes (both hanging offenses). In sentencing me, Justice Lamont indicated that, "while the robbery of Mister Farrell was accompanied by threats of violence designed to intimidate, no violence was actually employed, and there has been no evidence presented by Crown counsel to suggest that Finn's robbery was anything other than a single affair, driven by impulse.

Taking into consideration all of the evidence and the finding of guilty on the grand theft by robbery charge, I hereby sentence Patrick Finn to incarceration in the Tralee Gaol until such time as arrangements can be made to transport Mister Finn to America, under penalty of death by hanging should he ever return to Ireland." Captain Farrell had wanted me dead or in prison at hard labor for the rest of my days. It did not work out quite that way, and Farrell was livid, blaming Justice Lamont for being outmaneuvered and believing the crock of a story presented in my defense.

But imprisonment, then exile to America – that was pure shite as well! I was now off to one of the toughest prisons in all of Ireland (some called it the worst gaol in all of Europe) and would be there until I was shipped away overseas and then to live out my final days as an old man in the forests of America. The Tralee Gaol held mostly people (men and women) waiting for their trials, some debtors, and two cells were set aside for dangerous criminals. Likewise, individuals like me waiting on transportation over the horizon were housed there until a scheduled ship was ready to sail. The old gaol, built in the 1600s, was overcrowded, rat-infested, peopled by a few violent prisoners who pretty much ran the place, and jailers who liked to inflict punishments (like flogging) for the slightest administrative transgressions. The gaol sat half-suspended over the local river and contained no courtyard, so a great deal of time was spent sitting in a cold, dank, filthy cell.

The thing that made the gaol uncomfortable was its age, but its age was also its vulnerability. It was easy to slip out of the irons, the locks were easy to 'pick,' the guards so slovenly and uninterested in their duties that you had plenty of time to do whatever you pleased so long as you followed their basic rules. It did not take long for like-minded prisoners to conspire concerning an escape plan: one former coal miner among us indicated it would not be difficult to tunnel out of the prison over the river section. Work began immediately utilizing tools smuggled into the prison care of the local Whiteboys Association hoping to free some of their captured fellows. The tunneling went on for weeks. When the time was right and the escape plan was finally set in motion, I was able to once again 'pick' the locks on my leg irons and slip out of my manacles. On a moonlit evening, we made our move: we tunneled out a final section of dirt and rock close to the arch of the nearby bridge and burst through the outside wall. We remained in the shadows, and the various escapees headed off in multiple directions up and down the river. About a dozen prisoners, including one woman, disappeared into the night. Now I was out. I was gone. I was free.

It was time for a reckoning.

11. A Thirst For Vengeance (Part 1)

GALWAY CITY, 1ST OF APRIL 1765.

Two people were responsible for sending me to that god-forsaken hole of a gaol in Tralee and ultimately for my planned transportation to America - Ginny O'Neill and Captain Farrell. Both must pay. But first, I must lay quiet for a while and acquire some measure of wealth. I could not immediately return to highway thievery and must maintain a staid lifestyle as I bided my time. I adopted a new name and character – "Terrence Murphy" – and returned to my coopers' roots. I moved north to Galway City in the far west, walking most of the way.

Galway ("Dun Gaillimhe" in Irish) was a Gaelic town that grew up around the fortifications of the Irish King of Connacht. Still, as time went by, it was dominated by its merchant families – the so-called "Tribes of Galway" – and became a key trading center with access to Galway Bay. First Norman, then English, control widened the divide between this trading city and the surrounding Irish country clans. At one time, town law forbade unfettered access by the Catholic country Irish into the town, proclaiming "...neither 'O' or 'Mac' shall struttle nor swagger through the streets of Galway..." without permission. Ironically though, the town thrived on trade with Catholic France and Spain, like many other west coast ports. When Gaelic power increased in Ireland, the city sided with the powerful but then paid a heavy price when first Cromwell, then later

William, brought the city to heel. The "Tribes" lost their influence, but the overseas trading connections that they had forged with the continent remained strong. The surrounding countryside retained its Irish culture, language, and traditions.

I found an opportunity to practice my cooper's trade at "Burke's Cooperage" during the day, found a room to rent in a private home, and started to explore the more 'sordid' side of Galway at night, especially its access to smuggled goods. I finally came across a gang of local ne'er-do-wells who called themselves "Queen Maeve's Children," based on some ancient Irish tale. In fact, I had to fist-fight the leader of the group, a Seamus O'Flaherty, in order to gain some measure of trust and acceptance with the gang. I lost the fight but gave a good enough account of myself that they were suitably impressed. O'Flaherty was not merely a brawler but a jokester and a jester as well. He, too, liked his beer and whiskey, and we struck up a friendship around that shared passion. However, it was also clear that O'Flaherty and his crew could get me what I needed, as with Boyer, my quest was once again for powder and a pistol.

"Why do you need a pistol when a knife will serve you just as well on these rough streets?" O'Flaherty asked. I replied, "Because I am both a 'pursuer' of those who have abused me and I am being 'pursued' by the British. I must be ready at any time to defend myself at both close range and at a longer distance from well-armed foes." The criminal leader nodded in agreement. After several months, O'Flaherty and the "Children" were able to fulfill my request for a firearm, but it cost me half my wages. As for Boyer, I found out during my time in Galway that he was tried and hanged by a military tribunal in Killarney for being a French spy. Ginny had caused the death of a man whose life she simply bargained away in her quest for gold and jewels.

I kept to myself, away from the public houses and crowded places in Galway, in order not to draw attention to myself. I was an escaped prisoner and had no intention of going back to Tralee or any other stone coffin of a prison to await transportation to the American colonies. However, the time was rapidly approaching when I would have to seek out my former bedmate and my tax-collecting nemesis for retribution.

Both would have to be dispatched in a manner that caused them the most shock, distress, and pain. I resolved on a general plan for each and started to put together the elements of those plans. Ginny O'Neill would be first.

Once I had purchased a horse (that I named "Boru"), gave my notice at the coopers, surrendered my tenancy, packed a small traveling bag, my pistol, powder, and cartridges, I then set off south to the wilder parts of coastal Ireland. This is where "Cailleacha" (witches), fairies, and leprechauns (little people) were thought to reside. Even my father – strong Catholic that he was – talked of the wild west coast and the incredible creatures that dwelled there with a certain reverence. It was a land where both the 'white' and 'black' arts were practiced, poisons mixed, and spells cast. In many ways, the west coast represented old Gaelic Ireland in its purest form.

I first went to the town of Ennis, a historic seat of the O'Brien dynasty, and, ironically, given the name of my horse, the descendants of Brian Boru, an Irish king. There I made subtle inquiries as to where I might find a "Cailleach" to confer with about my future prospects (not really). I was directed to an old woman who lived in the fishing village of Kilkee to the southwest. As Ennis was a military town with many soldiers about, I quickly set off in the direction of Kilkee, which was also within a reasonable distance from Limerick.

The old woman's name was Deirdre Moloney, and townsfolk in Kilkee pointed me toward her small cottage on the outskirts of the village. It sat in an isolated location full of tangled brush and buffeted by strong coastal winds. She was at home when I arrived, and, lucky for me, she spoke good English, as many inhabitants of these parts spoke only Irish. She invited me into her cottage for a cup of tea made from wild roots, served beside a burning turf fire in her stone fireplace. She sat in her rocker, lit up a pipe, and struck a stern demeanor.

"What is it you are looking for from me, sir?" Deirdre asked. I sat on a stool across from her and told her in some detail about my early life, how I had been betrayed by my partner, jailed, stripped of all that I owned, and had a good friend hanged as a consequence of my partner's perfidy. "So, it is vengeance that you seek?" she asked. "Yes, indeed," I replied.

Then she said, "If I agree to help you and resort to the use of the 'black arts,' you must realize that the consequences of that resort cannot be anticipated or controlled. Once such forces are unleashed, they might even destroy the one they were meant to benefit." I said, "Provided my thirst for vengeance is satisfied, consequences be damned." She then indicated, "I will help you as the powers that I hold tell me that you speak the truth. You have been done badly by your former lover, so much so, that another man has died as a result. One life must now be taken in substitution for that lost soul. I can collect together the necessary elements of a 'potion' that will ensure the demise of your former partner, and, together with the proper spell I will cast, you shall have your revenge. Would you be satisfied with such an outcome?" I said, "It is very much what I had in mind. What must I give you in return?" She replied, "An appropriate donation in order to satisfy the spirit world and further my ongoing assistance to others." In other words, money. We agreed on a satisfactory price, and she told me to return tomorrow in the late afternoon.

I had struck a bargain with a witch.

I spent the night in Kilkee at the only inn near the town, "The Wild Boar." The next day, at the appointed time, I went back to see the Cailleach and secure the "potion." The old woman smiled when I arrived and said, "I have made your vengeance potion from 'Himlic' (hemlock), and it will cause a fairly quick and painful death for your former lover. Administer it to her in her favored drink. I will cast the required spell when you leave here. Now it is time that I am paid." Right to the point, she was.

The witch's dues were paid, and I thanked her heartily. I took my leave, and now I must find Ginny. It was back to Killarney the next morning over the same mountain trails where I had first come across (and later robbed) Captain Farrell.

I tracked down Brendan O'Connor at the "Black Horse Inn" and gave him no indication that I suspected he had shared in Ginny's ill-gotten gains. I asked him where I might go to speak with Ginny and, seeing the pistol tucked in my belt, he nervously informed me that Ginny now owned a millinery shop in the town: barmaid to hatter – quite a change in trades! I could only imagine where Ginny got the resources to open her own hat shop.

O'Connor asked me how I had been released from prison before being transported to America. I concocted a story about how the prisons were so overcrowded that those convicts simply waiting to be sent overseas were being released into the population and were given a date to return to a designated port when their ship was ready to sail. O'Connor was skeptical and then got a concerned look on his face. He asked, "You do not plan to bring any harm to Ginny, do you?" I laughed and said, "Why would I do that? We were once the closest of friends and shared a bed. I learned at my trial that she only went to the authorities and said what she said to them out of fear upon learning from a patron at the inn that Farrell had already discovered where I might be residing. Worried that I would be killed in any surprise raid, she made a deal with the captain that rendered me harmless, as she stole away my rapier and destroyed my cartridges. She thus spared my life as Farrell and his men arrived ready for a fight. I owe her my very existence." O'Connor again looked very skeptical (given everything that he had already told me about Ginny's greedy motives for betraying me) but had already revealed to me her new place of business.

"In fact," I said, "let me buy a jar of whiskey from you to take to the loveliest barmaid – sorry, loveliest hatter – in all of Ireland." O'Connor fetched me the jar, I paid for it, and I departed from the inn for the millinery before his suspicions turned into a warning to the authorities about my possible intentions. I stopped in a secluded spot on my way to Ginny's shop in order to administer the Cailleach's "potion" to the jar of whiskey I had purchased.

I found Ginny's millinery in the center of Killarney and simply walked straight through the main door into her place of business – with the pistol tucked into my belt in an intimidating fashion in order to put her on edge and make her compliant. Ginny was there with her back to the street-side door serving a customer. I said, "Hello, my red-haired beauty." She turned toward me with a look of horror on her face. It was like a ghost had just returned from the dead to greet her. She replied, "My God! Mister Finn," then turned to her patron and asked, "Can we discuss your requirements later today, once I have had a chance to deal with this gentleman?" The patron cheerfully agreed and departed the place.

"Why are you here?" Ginny asked in a more somber tone. I replied, "Because I was anxious to have a friendly drink with my favorite person in all the world." She then said nervously, "And why the pistol?" I replied, "Self-defense. Killarney is a town where one can be snatched up off the street by the authorities with no just cause at any time."

Ginny questioned, "Have you come to harm me?" I replied, "Of course not. In fact, I have come to reward you. Your 'forgetfulness' at my trial probably kept me off the gallows; and we did live quite happily together – virtually as man and wife – since the 1750s, before all of this 'unpleasantness' occurred. A relationship like ours does not simply fall to pieces because of a series of bad decisions giving rise to the types of situations we each find ourselves in today." Ginny looked surprised and asked, "Do you plan to stay in Killarney? I thought that the court ordered you to go to the American colonies?" I answered, "Stay. Go. It is all the same to me now. But before I make any final decision about my future, I wanted to come and see you and offer you a drink in the spirit of our reconciliation."

You could see Ginny's mouth watering at the very sight of the whiskey. I asked her, "Do you have any cups here?" She replied, "There are goblets in a cupboard at the rear of the shop. I will show you." We passed through a curtain shielding the rear area from the front of the store, and Ginny retrieved two goblets from a cupboard. She said, "You know, I always enjoyed the time we spent together, and you were always very generous with me. I was wrong to have taken advantage of you in any way. Maybe we can even rekindle our affection for one another, here and now, as another sign of our reconciliation." I smiled and said, "Well, I can certainly drink to that prospect." I poured two cups of whiskey and raised my goblet, saying "Sláinte" (or "health" in Irish).

As usual, Ginny quickly slammed her drink back into her throat with a flourish. She had a puzzled look on her face immediately, however, and said, "Where did you get this whiskey?" I replied, "At the 'Black Horse Inn' from our good friend, Mister O'Connor. Why do you ask?" She screwed up her face and said, "It tastes bitter. What is in the jar?" I replied, "Death."

Ginny's face contorted. She started to sweat. As the minutes passed, she appeared wobbly. She grabbed the edge of a table to support herself, coughing and trying to catch her breath. "You have poisoned me!" she finally cried out. I shot back, "You poisoned my whole life with your greedy ways." Ginny attempted to reach a butcher's knife she had hidden beneath a piece of cloth on a shelf in the back room (which she may have thought to use on me at some point in time), but I drew my pistol and backed her away. As she doubled over in stomach pain from the effects of the hemlock, I whispered in a sing-song voice, "I never will deceive you. I never will betray you." Ginny screamed, "You bastard! I will see you in hell." I replied, "Yes, you will, but you will get there first." Weak and staggering about, she finally collapsed on the floor of the shop, breathing heavily in bursts and convulsing. She fell asleep and expired. It was a painful death, no doubt. Ginny would not have wanted to die that way. Ginny should not have betrayed me. Lesson learned.

I took the knife from Ginny's lifeless grasp and replaced it back under the cloth. I said to myself, "My, my, another suicide by an informer racked with guilt." I left her shop through a rear door. If O'Connor kept his own counsel (possibly fearful of retribution from me), then no one may even question Ginny's untimely demise. But I was an escaped prisoner on the run. Henceforth, traveling and hiding were my life, and there was still unfinished business: the oh-so-clever Captain Farrell was still on the loose, abusing the Irish population. And I planned to stop him.

12. A Thirst For Vengeance (Part 2)

OUTSIDE KILLARNEY, KERRY, 30TH OF OCTOBER 1765.

One dispatched; one more awaiting justice.

I slept on my bedroll on the cold, wet ground in the forests and on the hillsides around Killarney. I went each day to assess the ring of protection which surrounded Captain Farrell's estate just outside of Killarney proper using a military glass. Farrell's manor house was surrounded by armed footmen who also served as his 'household cavalry' whenever he traveled in the immediate area. It was almost as if he expected another attack on his person. Armed with carbines and sabers, his mounted footmen were a formidable little force, and with a single pistol and a limited supply of powder, I was not about to engage with them. In addition, when Farrell traveled beyond his estate, he now wore a personal set of twin pistols in crossed holsters over his chest. I did not know if he still traveled alone on his very 'taxing' duties beyond Killarney, but I could not wait until the captain decided to travel north to Tralee again, or elsewhere outside of Killarney. That would take time - time I did not really have - as British dragoons made periodic sweeps of the surrounding countryside (looking for me?). I must strike Farrell at a time and in a place he least expected it and soon - but where exactly?

Following him about for several weeks, I noticed that the captain went to the local "Hunt Club" in Killarney every Saturday afternoon in order to drink port, read the printed gazette, smoke a pipe, and talk with his loyalist cronies for several hours. He always removed his pistol belt whenever he entered the place. There was only one man on the door, behind a desk in the front entryway. I decided that this was where Farrell was most at ease (other than in his own home), was unarmed, and unsuspecting - perfect. I surveyed the club and found that alleyways radiated out from the rear kitchen and delivery area and were obviously my best escape routes. On the appointed Saturday, I followed Captain Farrell and his entourage of footmen to the "Hunt Club" where they temporarily parted ways. I rode "Boru" to the mouth of one of the alleyways, hitched him to a post, and made my way back to the front of the club. I entered the big chestnut doors, my cloak concealing my loaded pistol.

I had walked into the entryway of the club on one previous Saturday, simply to get a sense of the place and observe Farrell and his habits from afar, but not staying too long. On the anointed Saturday for my revenge, I went to the front desk and I asked the footman positioned there, "Excuse me, is Captain Farrell about?" "Yes," he said, "he is in the main salon at his usual table." I replied, "Might I have a word with him?" The footman shook his head and said, "Sorry, sir, only those who are members of the club are permitted in the principal areas. I do not recognize you as being a member, but I will take Captain Farrell a note if you like?" I could see Farrell sitting in a central location through the open salon doors. "Would you?" I asked. "Certainly, sir," the footman indicated. I replied, "Well, I have a message for him right here." I jerked out my pistol, butt end first, and slammed the footman sideways across his head. He dropped like a sack of flour. I then strode in a determined fashion across the half-empty salon, coming up quickly on the seated Farrell. He had his nose in his gazette and only turned to look at me at the last second as I cocked the hammer back on my pistol. His mouth dropped open in recognition. My heart was pounding. All I said to him was, "Hello, Captain." I shot him straight through his open mouth. His head twitched backward, then he slumped sideways in his chair, falling to the floor. I then proceeded through the club, walked past a number of startled members seated or half-seated in an inner salon, strolled past the servants and cooks in the kitchen, and then out the rear door. I turned right when I got outside, maneuvered down the alleyway I had selected earlier, mounted "Boru," and disappeared out of the town and into the hills. My work in Killarney was done, my revenge complete.

I collected my few belongings and moved quickly east toward Waterford, avoiding the main roads as much as possible. From Waterford, I journeyed north to Kilkenny, a delightful city on the route to Dublin. Kilkenny, known as "Cill Chainnigh" in Irish, in the province of Leinster, was built along the strategic River Nore. The city, like many other Gaelic centers, began as an ecclesiastical settlement and contained many churches and abbeys. It later became a bastion of Norman power and a merchant town with strong fortifications and a large castle. The place was so influential that it received a city charter from James I in the early 1600s but walked a fine line between protecting its acknowledged Irish-Norman heritage and status, while resisting growing English Protestant control. But like so many near-autonomous walled cities in Ireland, it joined a Catholic Confederation during the 1641 rebellion against the English and paid the price with a brutal siege by Cromwell in 1650. Kilkenny resisted valiantly, however, so much so that it only surrendered on honorable terms from the besiegers. The city revolted once again during the wars against William of Orange, with King James II making it his headquarters in the south during the winter of 1689-1690. My father and mother served in the ranks of the Irish army and its supporters during that time.

Kilkenny was a brewing center and had a need for coopers. I found work with a brewer, "Kilkenny Ales," in the 'Irish Town' section of the city and stayed at the hospitable "Governor's Inn," named in honor of Sir Walter Butler, the governor of the place during Cromwell's siege. While I was good at my trade, the highway still called out to me. Kilkenny sat in the important north-south corridor between Dublin and the rich southern Irish ports, although many travelers took the coastal route as well. The prosperous surrounding area had just enough traffic to make it a prized hunting ground. While I knew that the 'Ascendancy' were going wild trying to track down the murderer of Captain Farrell, right within the sanctity of a Loyalist club, I could not shake myself out of the allure of the road. It was easy money as far as I was concerned and as potent a passion as I once felt for Ginny; yet I had to be careful not to let complacency set in again. Like O'Boyle, I started to strive for ever-increasing levels of risk and reward, treating the intoxication of the robbery as normal, not extraordinary. I almost lived openly as a "Rapparee" at one time, hanging about with dangerous characters like Monsieur Boyer. Now it was time to live in the shadows, stay away from barmaids, avoid large crowds if possible - if I wanted to live at all after two murders, most notably the tax commissioner Farrell, the King's man.

I actually missed Ginny. I missed her gaiety when times were good, such as after the strike against Lord Duncan, and I missed her care and attention to me after the failed army pay wagon assault. Why did she have to betray me? I would have given her anything, everything; but she still wanted more. Ginny was too much her own woman with her own mind: she wanted what she wanted when she wanted it, and there was no dissuading her. But when 'want' turned to 'treachery,' I had to administer personal justice. She should have expected no less given the character and level of her betrayal.

Where to prudently make a strike now? It would have to be a "coins-only" raid for I had lost my receiver of stolen goods in Boyer. A number of merchant guilds maintained establishments in the city of Kilkenny and might make fine targets. But first, I returned to what I knew best — robbing coaches and carriages. I went roving in the local area, but after only two robberies, bearing modest profits, a series of raids and arrests by constables and the army exploded in Kilkenny, and I had to slip away in the dead of night to avoid arrest. The south of Ireland was becoming just too dangerous in the wake of Farrell's killing. Should I go north or try to leave Ireland entirely? I resolved on the former course of action as I had not come to my ancestral homeland just to be driven away by English loyalists. It is they who should fear me, not the other way around. I aimed for the city of Derry (called "Doire" in Irish) in the far north, some 70 leagues away.

I first struck out toward Dublin on good roads but veered to the northwest as the traffic nearer to the capital became heavy. I rode through the rolling hills of the north, sleeping again in the cold and wet of the countryside as I tried to avoid the highways in this Loyalist country. While the population was fairly balanced in terms of numbers, Catholic versus Protestant, each religious community generally lived separately and kept to themselves, with the cities mainly dominated politically, economically, and militarily by the Protestant population.

The province of Ulster in the north was once the greatest bastion of Catholic Ireland under the leadership of its powerful Earls. However, by the early 1600s, the Tudor English under Elizabeth I had broken that power and forced the Earls and their key supporters to flee to the continent. A wave of English land confiscations followed, and the wholesale English and Scottish Protestant colonization of the north of Ireland had begun. A population wholly loyal to Great Britain became embedded in the north, supported by William of Orange's victories over James II during the Siege of Derry (1689) and at the Battle of the Boyne (1690). Aided by the "Flight of the Wild Geese" Catholic militaries after the Treaty of Limerick (1691) and the "Penal Laws" brought in by the Irish Parliament and Protestant establishment, the Protestant hold on the north was pretty much assured. Yet, it was always contested by the Catholic Irish in both large and small ways.

The walled city of Derry, renamed "Londonderry" by James I in the early 1660s, originated like so many Irish towns and cities as a religious settlement. However, its important position on the River Foyle with access to the sea led to the London-based merchants who dominated its trade turning its west bank into a powerful, well-designed walled fortress, bristling with artillery. The city resisted many sieges, including the failed 1689 assault by James II. By the 1760s, the old walled city was a merchant's enclave protected by unbreached city walls with the English architecture of the Hanoverians dominating. This trading center with a busy port was surrounded by a countryside settled by a hostile Gaelic Catholic population, like so many other walled Irish merchant cities on the island.

After sensing a degree of hostility in the city itself (my southern Irish brogue standing out against the English and rough Scottish accents in that place) and after observing that the county roads were heavily patrolled by local militia and Irish (really, British) army units, I decided that this was no location for a Jacobite highwayman to ply his trade. I elected to move southeast to the Catholic market town of Kilrea, where I was less conspicuous (even though my accent still raised some eyebrows among the locals). Armed with the coopers' trade that had given me cover since arriving in Ireland, I found work with a local barrel maker, "Moffitt's Coopers," under the false name of "Liam McGrath," which I had utilized in Kilkenny. Ironically, I settled into residence at an inn called "O'Neill's" and renewed my correspondence with Erin in France – possibly a dangerous move for an escaped prisoner-murderer on the run to make. But no matter: life was dangerous. You could step out into the road and be run down by a speeding coach. Everything, every minute of life, was a gamble. Some win the gamble, some lose.

Erin wrote to me by return post periodically, although the mail was tardy. In early 1766, she informed me in an unexpected piece of correspondence that John was finally back in Ireland! The 40th Regiment of Foot had been relocated from America in 1764. I had longed to be reunited with my brother and had searched for him in vain in both Cork and in Killarney. I wrote to her in haste to see if she could discover his exact whereabouts. I began to think that if there was anyone who could help me out of my dilemma as a man on the run, it was my brother in the army. I even dreamed that someday we could join one another in civilian life, roving the countryside, maybe around the fine town of Kilkenny that I was forced to abandon earlier. But first, I must find him. Erin finally reported that she heard through their mutual friends that John was not stationed in either Cork or in Killarney but was in Dublin.

It was time to go to Ireland's capital – the first city of the land.

13. Dublin

DUBLIN CITY, 4TH OF JUNE 1766.

Beautiful carriages rolled by, youth playing traditional Irish sports in the city's parklands (although such Gaelic sports were frowned upon by the authorities), plenty of places to drink beer and whiskey or watch the fair maids of the capital stroll by in the morning - this was Dublin. Like Derry, it bore all the hallmarks of the types of architecture and city planning favored by England's kings: wide thoroughfares, imposing stone buildings (especially government structures), green public spaces, robust trade and commerce along the city's Liffey River waterfront. In a word, "impressive." But Dublin was not always this way.

Like so many coastal towns and cities in Ireland, the small Gaelic settlement at Dublin (or "Baile Átha Cliath" in Irish) really came into its own as a Norse trading center, with allegedly the largest slave market in all of Europe. The Norse remained and blended in with the local Irish population even after their defeat by Irish King Brian Boru near Dublin at the pivotal Battle of Clontarf in 1014. But then came the Normans – French descendants of the Norse who successfully invaded England in 1066. They captured Dublin in the 1100s and made Dublin Castle the center of power for their government. Norman power and influence were, however, mostly limited to the coastal strip of land known as the "Pale," and Dublin itself endured uprisings, sieges, and the "Black Death" plague. By the time of Cromwell's invasion of Ireland in the 1600s, the capital was reportedly a medieval shambles in decline. But better days were ahead: an influx of Protestant weavers fleeing the continent made Dublin a center of the cloth trade, and the economy boomed. Dublin was transformed into a fashionable and elegant city by the English in the mid-1700s. This was the Dublin I was being exposed to.

The army establishment in Dublin was headquartered in the so-called "Royal Barracks." It was an imposing stone building located at Arbour or "Arbhair" (Corn) Hill in Dublin, and where my search for brother John would begin. The barracks were designed to not only house the army (avoiding billeting on the population and some unpleasant 'mixing' - that is, an excessive resort to whoring, gambling, drinking, fighting with street gangs, dealing with unruly crowds) but to overawe a majority Catholic population prone to insurrection, just as the other government, educational, and Church of Ireland landmarks in the capital were designed to do: architecture that was all about reinforcing the supremacy of the Protestant establishment.

Built around 1701, the "Royal Barracks," sometimes simply called "the Barracks," was a massive place featuring several large squares directed south and was faced with granite. The place could hold hundreds of troops at a time from among the thousands stationed in Dublin over the decades. The surrounding area became a fine example of the degradation of the Irish poor brought about by the British occupation: it featured a host of brothels and public houses serving any soldiers with coins in their pockets and was populated by all forms of thieves, whores, rogues, and beggars intent on separating soldiers from their money.

I went to the "Royal Barracks" and was able to find a sergeant who was familiar with the 40th Regiment of Foot. When I inquired after John, he asked, "And you are?" I replied, "Michael Mackin, his best friend growing up, come from London," (which was all true, in terms of Michael). He then confirmed to me that there was a "Lieutenant Finn" who served with that regiment. The 40th was currently on maneuvers, featuring extensive marching, weapons, and formation drills, building camps, and mock battles. "It will be four or five days before they are back here," the sergeant said. I thanked him and quickly slipped away from this barracks full of soldiers, heading into Dublin.

Dublin was still in the midst of a massive transformation when I arrived, shifting from a medieval city to an English showplace. The Liffey River had ceased to be used as an open sewer and was now a highway of commerce, with planned canals radiating out to the Shannon River in the south and the Irish Sea in the north. Streets on both sides of the river were being widened, and new residential homes were under construction, especially on the north side. On the south side of the river, a new large brewery was being built, with the relevant land leased for a legendary 9,000 years. Even Dublin Castle was undergoing some transformation, evolving from a military and government stronghold into more of a residence and reception place for officials like Britain's Lord Deputy, their Chief Governor in Ireland. I walked past the Irish Parliament building on College Green and turned to see the impressive Trinity College façade. I thought to myself, this whole area is a 'façade' – a parliament where the members of the majority population could not sit, an institution of higher learning that they could not attend, churches where they could not worship, and houses they could not own – a mere façade of "Saoirse" (or "freedom" in English).

I took a room at an inn on Lower Bridge Street, once a residential area but now transitioning into more of a commercial area. I returned to the Royal Barracks on the appointed days and was finally told by a sentry that the 40th Regiment was on route. I waited near the main gate, and eventually, the men of the regiment arrived, marching with flags flying, drums beating, and fifes whistling. Their battle flag bore the streamers of victories in America: Louisbourg, Quebec, Havana. After a few minutes, I recognized John in command of his 30 or more soldiers. I don't think he saw me at first, not until he was told to "fall out" - then he saw me and embraced me in recognition. "My God, Patrick, you are an old man!" he laughed. "Not as old as you," I replied, also laughing. "Where did you come from, brother?" he asked. I replied, "I have been working as a cooper mostly in the south of Ireland since 1748." He laughed once again and said, "Guess those barrel-making skills you learned back on the estate finally proved their worth!" I asked, "Are you able to come for a drink?" He replied, "If you can wait here, I only have to stow my gear, and I will be back. Maybe half an hour?" I agreed. The sergeant who I originally encountered when first coming to the barracks had been hovering around the reunion with my brother. He gave me a strange look then disappeared into the barracks.

As promised, John was quickly back with me, and we headed off to find a public house. John suggested the "Hole in the Wall" as a good spot, a place popular with the army (and, ironically, once called the "Blackhorse Inn"), but we had to hire a coach to get us there. En route, John talked about life in the army and his adventures overseas. I asked him if he knew that we faced each other at Culloden. He said no, that was news he had not heard before. He left it at that, not willing to broach the subject of our clash any further. I then asked him if he stayed in touch with Erin at all. He replied that they only kept in touch through friends, like Michael Mackin, a boyhood chum (who I had impersonated with John's sergeant), but not directly. He then said, "I heard that you had to provide Erin with some 'assistance' with the estate a while back." I said yes. He asked, "What form of assistance?" I replied that her worthless husband and his 'friends' had to be driven off the estate, and Erin put back in the position of mistress of the chateau. John let that topic go as well. I received the distinct impression that he was wholly uninterested in most aspects associated with his former adult life in France. Finally, we arrived at the public house, and we went in for some liquid refreshment. The place was full of British soldiers, which made me uncomfortable, but I tried not to show that discomfort to John.

Before long, the porter and whiskey were flowing freely, and our tongues were sufficiently loosened. We reminisced at first about our close bond as boys playing at being Irish heroes on our family's estate in France. But then John changed the subject suddenly. "So, where did you say you lived after coming to Ireland?" John asked. I said, "Cork and then Killarney mostly." He replied, "Ah, the rebel south. I was stationed there for a while and had to deal with my share of Jacobite traitors and murderers." I winced a bit and said in a low voice, "Well, maybe they had their reasons to murder." John shot back, "You mean like you and Father had your reasons to fight for the greatest Papist tyrants the world has ever known – Louis XIV and XV?" I then retorted, "You mean tyrants like the butcher Cromwell who spared neither woman nor child as he raped Ireland or William of Orange, who drove our family and thousands more like us from our lands and heritage?" With his voice raising a bit, he said, "What heritage? Priest-ridden slavery overseen by barbaric kings and earls who bowed to Rome, rather than subjects ruled over by enlightened monarchs directed by a freemen's parliament and advised by men of science and letters?" I replied, "Yes, I have seen your 'freemen's parliament' that allows only freemen of the national church to sit in it and your enlightened rulers who have to keep power at the point of a bayonet."

John quickly downed another whiskey and scowled. He asked, "Why did my sergeant come to me and say you misled him as to who you were?". I questioned, "What do you mean?" He said, "You presented yourself to him as 'Micheal', a childhood friend; but later he heard me call you 'Patrick' and 'brother'. Why lie?" I replied, "Your sergeant needs to keep away from private conversations and mind his own affairs." John said in a rough tone, "Answer the question." I replied, "Who are you, my interrogator? You have served far too long in an army of occupation that berates and oppresses our people." He shot back, "You mean saves our people from the clutches of savage Catholic insurgents and highwaymen who plague our countryside and force the common people to live in fear." I did not like where this conversation was headed. "Time for us to go," I said. He then replied in an accusatory voice, "After my conversation with my sergeant, I took the time to look at the broadsides advertising rewards for rebels. It seems that a prisoner named 'Patrick Finn' escaped from the Tralee Gaol before being transported to America on an armed robbery conviction. He is also now wanted for questioning in the death of a Killarney female shopkeeper and an area landowner shot to death while quietly sitting at his club. You would not know who they are talking about, would you?" I declared, "Not in the least. Time to go," and stood up. My own brother was trying to ensnare me. I would not play his game.

We caught a coach and said nothing on our return trip. I was dropped off at my inn while John continued on to the barracks. We never said goodbye to each other. It was clear to me that John had not changed in the least in all these years – still quick to let his opinions get in the way of happy family relations. I once dreamt of John finally leaving the army and going roving about with me in the south of Ireland. Now, that appeared unlikely. Maybe our most recent reunion was a bad idea entirely.

I spent the next day simply wandering about Dublin, stopping in at several quayside public houses to have a drink or two. I resolved to leave Dublin and head somewhere more secure. But where? Maybe it was finally time to head to Cork and catch a ship to France. I loved Ireland, but it did not seem that 'British' Ireland loved me much. Everyone I came with or met with seemed to end up dead – some by my own hand. And now I had a brother who would not be reconciled with me.

That night I lay down to sleep in my chamber; but just before slumber found me, I saw the flickering of torches outside of my window. I rose to look outside, and the street was crowded with British soldiers. I knew immediately that they were after me. I threw on my shirt and breeches and in a repeat of my escape attempt from the "Black Horse Inn", I bolted for a rear window across the building. I was only on the second floor, so I reasoned that I could drop down to the ground hanging from the second-floor windowsill above. I had no pistol with me but hoped that I could reach my horse, "Boru," in the livery area where my pistol was stored; but it was not to be. As I crumpled to the ground, I looked up to see a ring of British bayonets around me. I was their prisoner – again.

I was carted off to the very center of British power in Ireland, Dublin Castle, to be questioned. It was by far the most brutal interrogation that I ever endured in Ireland. My eyes were both swollen nearly shut from beatings I received as they tried to pry information out of me about "Rapparee" activity in Ireland. At first, they not only threatened my life but told me that John would now be drummed out of the army and disgraced – unless I talked; but talk about what, exactly? I had never been part of an organized ring of rebels striking the British. I was always a 'lone wolf,' so to speak, except when I rode with O'Boyle. What about

Ginny's death, they asked? What was the reason behind it? Was she killed in retaliation for informing to the authorities? Who was involved in the shooting of Captain Farrell? Were "Whiteboy" plotters involved in the murder, and were other Crown officials in danger of assassination? I could only tell them what I knew: it was me and always me alone. They never believed me and tried to beat the truth from me; and I thought in the meantime, how had I been betrayed? Was it a suspicious innkeeper? Was it that nosy sergeant from the Royal Barracks? As my interrogators changed tactics and softened their approach with me somewhat, I bluntly asked them: Who was it that betrayed me? They laughed at me. My chief inquisitor said, "What, you do not know? You were betrayed by your own brother."

Once again, I could not comprehend the information I had just received. My own brother? Really? We had pledged as boys to always support one another - to always have one another's "back" – but now the bonds of trust forged in France were wholly broken. Still, I must hear the betrayal from John's own lips. I told my interrogators that I would tell all I had to tell about "Rapparees," but to John alone. They quickly agreed, and the next day John came to my holding cell at Dublin Castle. I was sitting on a masonry ledge in the cell, hanging my head when he arrived. I hardly looked up when he first entered the cell.

"Heartless serpent," I said. He stood looking down at me, obviously proud of what he had done, and replied, "I have no time or mercy for Jacobite traitors regardless of who they might be." I said, "Even your own brother?" He replied, "Especially my own brother!" I shook my head and declared, "Father was right about you all along, and I should have listened to him and never trusted you." He shot back, "It is you and Father who broke the most fundamental of trusts, traitors to your legitimate sovereigns and kingdom." I said, "The pretenders William and the various George's will never be my kings, and England, or an occupied Ireland, will never be my kingdom. Éirinn go brách." He laughed and said, "You traitors disgust me. Fake Irishmen who yearn for a Gaelic nation and past that never really existed. This talk is pointless – unless you want to save yourself by telling me everything."

It was time. I was tired. I told him everything, whether it would save me or not: the attack on the manor house, the highway robberies, including the one involving Lord Duncan, the army pay wagon attack, the robbery - then killing - of Farrell, and finally, Ginny's murder.

He declared, "I cannot believe it. You treacherous Catholic dog. You have been involved in so much treason it will be difficult to sort through and catalogue it all. It simply defies all reason. You are no bother of mine but simply a rogue, scoundrel, and murderer." I replied, "And you are certainly no brother of mine. Go lick your English king's arse." John stormed out. I would not see him again until my trial. I was kept in the County of Dublin Gaol, a smelly dungeon near the Kilmainham Army Hospital, before being moved into Dublin proper pending my trial. I quickly surmised that "telling everything" to John would not save me. The end was coming.

14. The End Times

DUBLIN CITY, 2ND OF SEPTEMBER 1766.

I was held at the Newgate Prison pending my trial before the Dublin Commission Court. Dublin had no Assizes; it was this high court that dealt with the most serious criminal offenses in the capital, such as high treason. "Newgate" was once one of the original gates in Dublin's city walls, now turned into a jail, and it was a vile place - men, women, and children, debtors, robbers, murderers, and lunatics jammed together, sometimes ten or more to a cell, stealing from one another, fighting over food, and assaulting one another. I think it was even worse than the Tralee Gaol, if that was possible. I was taken back and forth from there to the "Tholsel" building on Skinners Row where the Commission Court sat.

Indicted once more on the charge of high treason, and now also murder and escaping custody, I faced the gallows if convicted.

The "Tholsel" building was one of the most important structures in medieval Dublin, serving as a combination city assembly hall, guildhall, court, and sometimes gaol. Close to Dublin Castle, it was a community focal point and featured the first public clock in all of Ireland in its tower dating from the 1400s. The Irish Parliament once sat there, but it was now home to the Commission Court, a court consisting of justices of the King's Bench.

At my trial, John, my brother, was to serve as my chief accuser and confessor, and he detailed my crimes before the court in a controlled and impersonal manner. You would think that he had never set eyes on me in his life before this trial: he detailed my many robberies, murders, and my assistance provided to Monsieur Boyer in aid of a planned insurrection – just as I had laid it all out to him at Dublin Castle. I was, of course, roundly convicted on all charges, despite a passionate defense from my counselor, Mister Elgin. He wholly condemned the use of torture to secure confessions, from me in particular and Irish prisoners in general, such confessions being inherently unreliable. But the jury of "freeborn good Protestant men," property owners, and men of substance all were oblivious to the evils of using torture to obtain confessions from alleged Irish traitors and were apparently swayed by the cool delivery of the seemingly impartial evidence given against me from a member of an "old and bold" British Army regiment – who happened to be my own brother. The portrait he painted of a ruthless Jacobite highwayman, who had terrorized the wealthy, stooped so low as to poison a female shopkeeper and murdered a Crown official, was, no doubt, compelling to them. I was doomed from the start and sentenced to be executed. I would be taken to Harold's Cross Green and, in the words of the presiding justice, Lord Dalton, be "hanged by the neck until you are dead."

John tried to visit me once as I sat in my Newgate Prison cell waiting for the implementation of my sentence, but I refused to see him. What was the point?

On a cold winter's day in early 1767, I was taken from my prison by ox cart under heavy guard to the public gallows at Harold's Cross ("Cros Araild" in Irish). A gallows had long been maintained at the Green, as a place to weigh goods coming into Dublin, as a toll collection point, and, of course, as an execution site. The spot was a key entry point to the city from the south along an important medieval road. On arriving at the Green, I was viewed by a large, slightly unruly, drunken, and bloodthirsty crowd of onlookers. Some carried bags of rotten vegetables with them, which they promptly threw at me as my cart approached the Green. I sat on my own coffin (provided by the county) in the cart. I was considerably demonized by court crime reporters as a result of my trial, and thus few in the crowd saw me as an 'Irish rebel' or any sort of hero: rogue, thief, killer of women and those victims, like Captain Farrell, taken unawares and unable to defend themselves – good riddance to me. My mother's words back in France that last day that we talked kept echoing in my mind and haunting me: "Misery and death awaits you in that country." The other words which kept coming back to me were those of the "Cailleach" of Kilkee, who told me that once the "black arts" were unleashed their consequences could not be predicted or controlled and may even destroy those they were meant to assist – and I was about to be "destroyed."

The hangman finally arrived along with an apprentice, a sheriff, and a government-approved priest. The hangman checked the sufficiency of the "short drop" on the gallows while the sheriff watched from the side on the execution platform. The hangman brought his own rope with him and ensured the noose was properly tied so that it would strangle me within a reasonable time – maybe ten to twenty minutes. A cold rain started to fall as I was brought to the platform. My hands were tied in front of me so that I could pray – too late for prayer to assist me much now! I scanned the crowd for any sign of John, just as I had done on the battlefield at Culloden, but I did not see him. It was best that he did not attend in any case.

The priest asked me if I wanted to pray a final prayer, and I silently obliged. The hangman then asked if I had any final words to say. I screamed out, "Death to all those who are opposed to a free Ireland." The crowd murmured a bit as if they were uncomfortable with my message. Then the noose was fitted about my neck.

While I had, at times, lived a very good and exciting life – especially with Ginny in the early days, or in the midst of a dangerous robbery - the betrayals by my lover and my brother were simply too much for me to bear any longer. My heart physically hurt with thoughts of their treason, but I did still love my sister in France, and I did love Ireland, its beauty, history, and especially its people. I loved my whiskey, but it clearly made me a fool on many occasions! Now it was time to step away from this cruel world and ride the highways of the great beyond, stopping now and then for a jar of that "water of life," that fruit of the barley.

Adieu. Slán. Goodbye.